PLATE OF POISON

Joe squirmed slightly as something light and feathery tickled the side of his arm.

"Don't move," Frank commanded, slowly rising to his feet. He fixed his eyes on the four-inch-long scorpion scurrying up his brother's bare flesh.

"What is it?" Joe asked. Then, as he glanced down and saw the venomous scorpion's segmented body, every muscle in his body tensed. "Get . . . rid . . . of . . . it," he told Frank through clenched teeth.

"Just don't move," Frank repeated, his fingers groping for a knife. He leaned over the table, holding the knife forward and stopped about six inches from Joe's arm. Now the scorpion was deadly still.

Suddenly the scorpion lashed its tail. Its poison stinger was poised—ready to plunge into Joe's outstretched arm!

Books in THE HARDY BOYS CASEFILES™ Series

Available from ARCHWAY Paperbacks

ROAD PIRATES

FRANKLIN W. DIXON

AN ARCHWAY PAPERBACK
Published by POCKET BOOKS
New York   London   Toronto   Sydney   Tokyo   Singapore

This book is a work of fiction. Names, characters, places and incidents are either the product of the author's imagination or are used fictitiously. Any resemblance to actual events or locales or persons, living or dead, is entirely coincidental.

AN ARCHWAY PAPERBACK *Original*

An Archway Paperback published by
POCKET BOOKS, a division of Simon & Schuster Inc.
1230 Avenue of the Americas, New York, NY 10020

ISBN: 0-671-73110-6

First Archway Paperback printing April 1993

10 9 8 7 6 5 4 3 2 1

THE HARDY BOYS, AN ARCHWAY PAPERBACK and colophon are registered trademarks of Simon & Schuster Inc.

THE HARDY BOYS CASEFILES is a trademark of Simon & Schuster Inc.

Cover art by Brian Kotzky

Printed in the U.S.A.

IL 6+

Chapter

1

"SLOW DOWN, JOE!" Frank Hardy called out over the roar of the wind.

"Just as soon as I pass this guy," Joe shouted back. He revved up the engine of the Porsche 911 convertible and pulled into the passing lane, trying to avoid the potholes on New York City's crowded Cross Bronx Expressway.

"Man, I wish we had this baby on a track," Joe called, his blue eyes bright with excitement. "She could really move out then."

"Take it easy! Don't go over the speed limit." Frank eyed the speedometer in the center of the dashboard. "We're here to nab crooks, not get a ticket."

Joe laughed, shrugging off his older brother's concerns. Eighteen-year-old Frank Hardy was al-

1

ways telling him what to do, Joe reflected, but this vacation there was no way his brother would keep him from having fun. It had been Joe's idea to spend spring break helping their father, Fenton Hardy, solve a case for Fenton's old friend, luxury car dealer Marty Hausman.

Over the past few months half a dozen of Hausman's cars had been stolen shortly after leaving his lot in Yonkers, New York, a few miles north of New York City. The thieves would pull the vehicles over, force the drivers out at gunpoint, then drive off in the cars. Hausman's dealership was not the only one affected. Thieves had been plaguing new car buyers throughout the New York City region. Now Hausman was convinced that news of the thefts was scaring away possible buyers.

Joe glanced over at Frank, whose dark hair was plastered flat to his head by the rushing wind. It had been Frank's idea to borrow one of Hausman's cars and drive around New York City, hoping the hijackers would target them. He had hoped to catch the car thieves red-handed.

"Watch out!" Frank shouted, turning deathly pale. Joe's gaze whipped to the front again, in time to see that traffic had almost stopped directly in front of them. Slamming on the brakes, he sent the Porsche into a slight skid. While he straightened it out again, Joe could feel Frank's accusing gaze boring into the side of his head.

"Okay, buddy," Joe heard Frank say as the Porsche slowed to a crawl behind a rusty blue station wagon. A child facing out the rear window was staring wide-eyed at Frank and Joe. "It's eight o'clock—time to switch places. My turn at the wheel."

"No way," Joe groaned, brushing his blond hair back out of his eyes. It was just after sundown on a warm April evening. On both sides of the highway the lights of New York's battered housing tenements rose against a purple sky.

"We'll be crossing the George Washington Bridge in a few minutes," Joe pleaded. "After that, we are out of New York and on the New Jersey Turnpike. That's four lanes of road with less traffic. I could get this bad boy out of second gear there."

"That's what I'm afraid of," Frank said sternly. "Don't forget, Dad's supposed to stay right behind us. What if the hijackers pull us over and he's not there?"

Frank was interrupted by a beeping sound. Joe glanced down at the cellular phone installed between the two bucket seats. "Speaking of Dad," he said. "You get it, Frank. I don't think I want to hear this."

Joe didn't have a choice. "Tell him to slow down!" a tinny voice bellowed over the phone. "I'm miles behind you and losing ground!"

Joe saw Frank grimace. "We read you, Dad," Frank said, glaring at his brother. "Joe was just having a little fun."

Fenton's next words were garbled as the car passed under a series of wide overpasses, blocking the cellular transmission.

"What'd he say?" Joe demanded.

Frank listened again, then said, "He says maybe we should pull over and wait for him. He lost us about ten minutes ago."

"Okay," Joe said with a sigh. "We'll pull over once we're over the bridge and in New Jersey. Then you can take over the wheel."

Frank listened to the phone again, then hung up. "Dad's going to check in with Hausman," he told Joe. "He says we'll keep driving till midnight, then call it a day."

"Fine with me." Joe glanced at a car full of teenage girls passing in the right lane. Several of the girls waved at the Hardys, obviously admiring the car. Joe tossed them a casual wave and pressed the accelerator, passing them instead. "Man, it hurts to think of a car like this getting stolen and chopped up for parts," he said to Frank.

"What makes you so sure a chop shop operation is hijacking these cars?" Frank asked. "Those guys usually steal parked cars—the risk is small. These hijackers are using guns. That means if they get caught, they'll be arrested for armed robbery, not just grand theft."

"You're right," Joe said. "Taking chances like that must mean the hijackers are getting more money than a chop shop could pay," Joe decided. "They must be selling these cars all in one piece, as is."

Frank nodded. "I can't figure out how they know where to find them, though," he said. "Do they stake out highways until new sports cars drive by or what?"

"If they do, I hope they're taking the day off," Joe remarked.

Just then Joe felt the car give a violent lurch forward.

"Hey," he snapped, peering into the rearview mirror. "Back off, Jack!"

"What's happening?" Frank spun around in the passenger seat.

"That big van just bumped us." Joe checked out the van in his rearview mirror. The tinted windows of the dark blue vehicle made it impossible to see the driver. Joe noted that the van was still close enough to rear-end the Porsche again.

"What's wrong with him? He's in some kind of hurry?" Joe demanded.

"I think there's more to it than that," Frank said, tightening his seat belt. "Get ready, Joe. These may be the guys we've been waiting for."

Joe's pulse lurched. He hadn't really expected an attack their first night out. He heard another crash as his head snapped forward. The van had rammed the rear of the sports car again. "That was no accident," he shouted, gripping the leather-covered steering wheel.

"Gun it!" Frank said, reaching for the cellular phone.

Joe mashed down the accelerator, and the sports car sprang forward, laying down rubber as Joe cut back into the left lane of traffic. Glancing in the rearview mirror, Joe saw that the van had sped up, too, and was keeping pace. "Hurry,"

Joe said to his brother as Frank pushed the speed dial button on the phone. "Get Dad!"

"It's busy," Frank shouted as Joe threaded his way through the heavy traffic.

"Great!" Joe cried. "He's checking in with Hausman—and we're about to check out!"

Just then, Joe heard the roar of a powerful new engine behind them. Glancing up at the rear-view mirror, he saw a beat-up old Chevy pull out from behind the speeding van. The car must have a powerful engine beneath its rusted hood, Joe realized. It was able to catch up with the Hardys in seconds.

Joe whipped the Porsche into the right lane, cutting off a shiny black Jeep, setting off a flurry of honking horns. Instantly the Chevy pulled even with the Porsche in the left lane. "Try Dad again!" Joe yelled at Frank.

"It's still busy," Frank shouted as the passenger window of the Chevy rolled down.

Joe faced straight ahead as the Chevy veered closer to the Porsche.

"Nice car, guys," yelled a voice from the station wagon. Joe glanced at the car. A young man in the passenger seat was leaning out the window, grinning from behind a pair of mirrored shades. "Pull over so we can take a look at it!"

"Take a hike!" Joe pressed harder on the accelerator. He glanced at Frank, who was speed-dialing Fenton again.

"I don't think so," the young man shouted, the Chevy keeping pace with the Porsche. "Pull over. Now!"

"Hello?" Joe heard Frank say into the phone. At that instant the Hardys passed under a wide set of overpasses. "I can't hear him," Frank shouted to Joe. "All I'm getting is static!"

Another car honked as it sped in the opposite direction. "I said, pull over!" the man in the Chevy demanded. "Now!"

Joe turned toward the Chevy and found himself staring into the barrel of a nine-millimeter automatic. "Uh-oh," he muttered, unable to take his eyes from the gaping black hole.

"You said it, buddy," the man in the sunglasses shouted.

Before Joe could respond, an explosion ripped through the air.

Chapter

2

"THAT WAS A warning shot!" the man behind the mirrored shades yelled. "The next one will splash your brains over the windshield!"

"Better do as he says, Joe," Frank said. For an instant he thought his brother had been shot.

"Take the exit!" the man in the shades yelled, pointing straight ahead at an exit ramp. It was blocked off with a row of widely spaced traffic cones and a Road Closed sign. As Joe hesitated, not sure what to do, cars veered sharply around them. "He wants us off the main road," Frank said, tense and staring straight ahead. "Maybe if you punch the accelerator, we could make a run for it off the ramp and lose them in local traffic."

"Okay," Joe replied, his knuckles white from

gripping the steering wheel. He guided the Porsche between the traffic cones. A moment later he groaned. "We're trapped," he said.

Frank followed Joe's gaze. The end of the ramp was blocked by a huge yellow- and black-striped barrier. There was no way out from there.

"We're on our own, Frank," Joe said.

"Keep cool," Frank responded nervously. "We'll think of something."

As Joe slowed the car to a stop, the Chevy darted in front of them and the van pulled up just inside the traffic cones. The ramp sloped sharply downhill, so no one could see the Porsche from the highway. The Road Closed barrier blocked off the view from the access road. Whatever happened here, Frank realized, there'd be no witnesses. Clearly these thieves had done this many times before.

"Now what?" Joe muttered as Frank twisted around to see two large men climb down from the van. The first, over six feet tall and enormously fat, placed a flare by the rear of the van and squatted by the rear tire with a jack, acting as though he were fixing a flat. The other man, a few inches shorter and a hundred pounds thinner with a head of snowy white hair, stood at the front of the van, his hand in his pocket and clearly holding a gun. Even if Fenton somehow guessed where his sons were, Frank realized, he'd never make it past the van to save them.

"We wait." Frank licked his lips nervously.

A door on the Chevy slammed shut and Frank

saw the man with the automatic coming toward them. In his early twenties and dressed in faded jeans and a denim jacket, the wiry young man swaggered up to Joe's door.

"Nice car, punk," the gunman said.

"Glad you like it," Joe replied coolly. "Now get lost."

The man grinned and pulled his gun from beneath his jacket. "It'd be a shame to mess up that fine leather upholstery, wouldn't it?" he said.

"What do you mean?" Joe said. Frank glanced down and saw that his brother was moving the gear shift. His pulse quickened as he realized what Joe was doing. He had slipped the car into reverse, his foot still on the clutch.

"You know what I mean. I want you to get out of the car nice and slow." The man opened the door for Joe. "I think I'll take it for a spin myself."

"Oh. Right." Joe turned to Frank.

"I guess we'd better do as the man says," Frank said, playing along.

Joe turned to get out of the car, but just then he jerked his foot from the clutch, hit the accelerator and ducked. Frank ducked, too, as the car careened backward up the hill, slamming into the white-haired gunman in front of the van. The car stalled as the man screamed and toppled over.

"Now!" Joe yelled as the young gunman ran toward them. Frank rolled out of the car as his brother opened his door even more, knocking it into the pursuing gunman's gut. From the edge of the ramp, Frank saw Joe leap out of the car and race to the shoulder of the highway near the front of the van. The young gunman was stumbling backward in Joe's direction, momentarily stunned.

"Joe! Are you all right?" Frank called, running toward his brother.

"Yes," Joe replied. "Let's get out of here!"

"Joe! Look out!" Frank screamed. He watched the young gunman leap for Joe. The thief had raised his gun barrel and now brought it down hard behind Joe's ear. "Joe!" Frank screamed as his younger brother slumped to the ground. Frank dove for cover behind the van as the hijacker spun around, his gun pointed at Frank.

The blast from the gun almost deafened Frank, who remained hidden behind the van.

If I can just hold on, Frank thought.

"Freeze!" bellowed a deep voice.

Frank raised his eyes into the barrel of yet another gun. The enormous man who had pretended to fix the flat stood with his pistol trained on Frank. The automatic seemed tiny in his beefy hand. Behind him the driver of the Chevy had gotten out of his car and was leveling a pistol at Frank, too.

"Nice try, kid," the fat man said with a grin. "Jackson!" he called over his shoulder. "Over here!"

The young man in the denim jacket came around from the front of the van.

"I say we waste these punks," the young man

said as he dragged Frank over to stand beside Joe, who was just opening his eyes.

"Don't be a mook," the fat man scoffed humorlessly. "The boss pays for cars, not corpses. You want to risk life in prison for murder, do it on your own time."

"Yeah, but J.R. don't want—"

"Shut up!" The fat man yelled.

Frank glanced over his shoulder at the fat man, who was clearly trying to gauge how much Frank had overheard. "We don't need strangers knowing our business," the fat man said.

Frank turned his back on the gunmen and helped Joe up after he heard the fat man grumble, "Get in the Porsche and drive. All of you—let's get out of here."

"Did you hear what I heard?" Frank whispered to his brother.

"Yeah. They're working for a guy named J.R." Joe stood rubbing his head as the fat man opened the sliding door on the van and helped the white-haired gunman into the rear seat. Then the fat man made his way around to the driver's side. Jackson climbed into the Porsche and gunned the engine as the Chevy driver began backing the old car up the ramp toward the highway.

"Wow," Joe said. "They act like we're not even here."

"We're not—to them," Frank pointed out. "They think we're ordinary civilians who just got the wits scared out of them.

"What's next?" Joe asked as the van roared off.

"We go up to the highway and hope Dad sees us. Then we try to come up with a way to explain how we let the car get stolen from us," Frank said.

"Do you have any idea how much a Porsche 911 costs?" Marty Hausman demanded of the Hardys an hour later as they sat facing him across his desk in his large, airy office in Yonkers. "I'll tell you how much. Probably more than your father earns in a year—and I don't think it was even insured."

"It has to be," Joe said, glancing nervously at his father. Joe turned back to Marty Hausman, who was now standing and staring out his window at a showroom full of gleaming European cars. "We were just taking it for a test drive, right, Frank? Your insurance policy must cover that."

"We do *not* send our luxury vehicles out for test drives on the Cross Bronx Expressway at eight o'clock at night," Hausman retorted, pulling himself up to his full five feet nine inches. Joe observed that the pudgy, white-haired man looked like a bantam rooster—if bantam roosters wore expensive suits.

"This is all your fault, Joe," Fenton said wearily. "You drove much too fast. If I'd been a hundred yards behind you as planned, we might have caught those hijackers and this case would be over. Instead, you almost got yourselves killed.''

"I'm sorry," Joe said as Marty Hausman popped his third aspirin since the Hardys had arrived. "I didn't realize I was so far ahead until it was too late.''

"Saying we're sorry won't replace the car,'' Fenton said. He turned to Hausman. "I don't know what to say, Marty, except that we'll stay on the case and won't quit until we've recovered your car.''

"What good will it do, Fenton?" Hausman waved off Fenton as though he were brushing aside a fly. "It must be chopped into tiny pieces by now. I don't sell parts,'' he added sulkily. "I sell cars.''

"But these cars can't be chopped up," Joe protested. His father and Hausman turned to him.

"Why's that?" Hausman asked.

"We were talking about it earlier,'' Frank explained. "We wondered why the thieves took such risks to hijack your cars and realized that the only way to make it pay was if they sold the cars whole. Then right before the hijackers drove away, one of them mentioned a boss named J.R. We heard him say J.R. pays for cars, not corpses.''

"Cars, huh?" Hausman turned away from the window, suddenly interested. "You mean whole cars—not parts?''

"What Frank says makes sense," Fenton told him. "This bunch of thieves would probably redo the cars, though—repaint them and change their serial numbers. Then they could resell them on the West Coast or overseas. That would explain why they seem to hijack only luxury cars—they'd earn the biggest profits for the hijackers.''

He turned to his sons. "Good thinking, boys. I'll tell the police to stop looking for car parts in chop shops and check out local warehouses and shipping companies instead.''

"That's still not much to go on," Joe said. "There must be thousands of warehouses around here.''

"It's all we have," Fenton answered.

"Hey, wait a minute," Frank interrupted. Joe turned to see Frank staring off into the distance. Joe knew that look—Frank had gotten an idea.

"I know how we can get more info about the thieves," Frank said.

"How?" Fenton asked.

"Simple." Frank glanced from Fenton to Marty Hausman. "We'll ask them," he said.

The others stared at him silently.

"Brilliant," Hausman finally said sarcastically. "Would you mind explaining, kid?"

"It's simple," Frank said with a glance at his brother. "We let our fingers do the walking."

Just then Joe caught on. He grinned at Frank as Marty Hausman and Fenton Hardy stared at each other in confusion.

"I get it, Frank," Joe said. "Dad, what was the number of the cellular phone in the Porsche?"

"Your phone?" Fenton asked. "It was 555-8421."

"Thanks," Frank said. "Mr. Hausman, may I use your phone? We're going to have a little chat with the bad guys."

Hausman moved toward the desk as Frank dialed the number. "You're calling the thieves? But—"

"Sssh!" Joe hissed. He held out a hand to stop the older man and watched as Frank held the phone to his ear. Joe grinned, impressed, as Frank's intelligent face became that of a hardened street punk.

"It's ringing," Frank said. The others waited in breathless silence as he listened for an answer.

Suddenly Joe heard a click from where he sat next to Frank. "Hello?" Frank said into the phone. Fenton and Hausman moved in closer to listen.

"Who is this?" came the reply. The voice was faint, but Joe could make out the words.

"You tell me first," Frank drawled with a wink at Joe. "Is this Jackson or the fat guy I'm talking to?" There came another pause.

"I'm big-boned—not fat," Joe heard the voice reply. "Call me Ambler. Now—who are you?"

Frank grinned at his brother. Joe couldn't believe their luck at finding the thieves still in the car.

"I'm Frank. Frank—Naylor. One of the guys you left to rot on the expressway," Frank said, adopting a harsh, street-punk tone. "I just want you to know, buddy—that wasn't my car you

16

stole. My partner, Joe, and I had just swiped it twenty minutes before you pinched it from us.''

"No kidding?" Ambler's voice said over the phone. "You've got some nerve, kid, calling to complain. What do you want—a receipt?"

"Nah," Frank drawled. "I want a piece of the action."

"A what?" the voice squawked as Fenton Hardy tried to grab the phone away. Frank turned his back and hunched over the receiver.

"I'm sick of swiping cars for chop shops and getting paid peanuts," he complained into the receiver. "There's no future in it, and I'm an ambitious guy. You know what I want, Ambler," he said with a glance over his shoulder at Joe. "I want to steal cars for J.R.!"

Chapter

3

FRANK LISTENED breathlessly for Ambler's reaction.

"I like your style, fella," he heard Ambler growl at last.

"Forget my style," Frank replied. "You guys play hardball, and I hear it pays."

Laughter came over the phone. "Yeah, we play hardball, all right," Ambler said. "This is the big leagues, kid. We are looking for new players, though, so I guess we could talk."

"With both of us," Frank said, nodding at Joe. "Or I don't play ball."

"Sure," Frank heard Ambler say. "That other guy's got guts. I almost had to laugh, the way he took down Jackson. You know the rest stop just

18

south of exit twenty-three on the Garden State Parkway?"

"Yeah, sure," Frank said, writing down the location.

"Meet me there at midnight," Ambler ordered. "Maybe we'll give you two a tryout. But I'm warning you, kid—I see one cop anywhere in the area and you and your partner are dead meat."

Frank slammed down the phone triumphantly. "Got him!" he said with a wide grin for his father. "Joe and I have a date at midnight to see if we're bad enough for this group of thieves."

"Good work, Frank," Fenton said dubiously, examining the sheet of paper on which Frank had written where and when he was to meet Ambler.

"I'll say," Hausman crowed, delighted. He clapped Frank on the back. "Everything I said before—forget. You boys are all right with me. All we have to do is send the cops to this rest stop and arrest the clowns. Case closed!"

"I'm afraid it's not that simple," Fenton warned. "You can't arrest people just for showing up at a rest stop."

"Don't worry, Dad," Frank assured him. "I have it figured out—Joe and I really have to join the thieves."

"Are you crazy?" Hausman demanded.

"No, it's perfect!" Joe said excitedly. "We'll join up long enough to find out where the cars are sent. Maybe we can even find enough evidence to nab J.R."

Fenton shook his head. "I don't like it," he said. "You'd both be taking too great a risk."

"Do you have a better idea, Dad?" Frank asked. "The way I see it, we owe Mr. Hausman a new Porsche unless we can get the old one back."

"You said yourself we need more evidence," Joe urged his father.

"Well, I guess it's worth a shot," Fenton said with obvious reluctance. He gave his younger son a stern look. "Meet with them, find out where their headquarters is, and that's it. You're out of there."

"Then it's settled." Hausman rubbed his hands with glee. "If there's anything I can do to help—"

"We do need one thing," Frank said.

"Name it," Hausman said.

"A Jaguar!" Joe cried eagerly.

"B-but—" Hausman sputtered.

"Don't worry. He's kidding," Frank said with a smile. "But we will need a car."

"A station wagon," Joe said with a groan as Frank steered the huge car slowly down the Garden State Parkway. "What car thief shows up in his aunt's station wagon?"

"Come on, it's not so bad." Frank chuckled.

Joe shook his head as Frank checked the rearview mirror. About seventy-five yards behind them he could see Fenton's car. They passed a sign beside the parkway that read Rest Stop—

One Mile. Beyond it were the lights of the rest stop's fast-food restaurant.

"Now remember—we're supposed to be professional car thieves hot to break into the big time," Frank reminded Joe. "Just play along with whatever happens until we get what we need."

"Right," Joe said. "Those guys won round one. Now it's our turn."

Frank parked the car in the middle of the lot. He turned to Joe and nodded toward the far end of the lot. "Look familiar?" he asked. Parked there was the dark blue van.

"Let's do it," he said.

As the two brothers crossed the lot, Frank concentrated on looking tough, carefully ignoring the car that pulled up and parked between their car and the van. He heard a car door open and shut, knowing that his father was walking up to a nearby pay phone. They had decided he would keep an eye on their meeting from there.

As the Hardys approached the van, the side door slid open. Jackson—still wearing his mirrored shades—stuck his head out.

"Oh, man," he said, "what do we want with these kids? They're a couple of Eagle Scouts."

"I *am* an Eagle Scout," Joe retorted. "My last merit badge was for beating up wise guys."

"Ha!" Frank heard Ambler's bark of a laugh from inside the van. "Get in here, kids."

Frank stopped, glancing at his brother. "Get in—now," Jackson snarled. "You want to be a part of this, you have to go through the initiation."

Frank hesitated. They had decided not to go anywhere Fenton couldn't see them. Frank studied Jackson's face and realized there would be no stalling. He climbed aboard the van, followed by Joe.

Inside, Jackson signaled for them to sit behind the front seat beside him.

"Welcome aboard, fellows," Ambler boomed as Jackson slammed the door shut. Ambler had turned around in the front passenger seat to greet them. "Drive," he ordered the white-haired man seated next to him.

"Drive?" Frank asked nervously. "Where are we going?"

"The land of opportunity," Ambler said.

The engine roared to life. As the van sped out of the rest stop, Frank saw Fenton scramble from the phone booth and head for his car. Frank knew there was no way he could catch up with them now.

"What do you want with these kids?" Jackson asked his partner. "Ambler, they must be fifteen years old."

"They have experience, right, guys?" Ambler said. "Come on, satisfy our curiosity. Tell us how many cars you've done."

"Well, after you lifted the Porsche from us, we stole the wagon we left at the rest stop. Two cars—I guess that's a typical day's haul," Joe answered, next to Jackson.

"What chop shops do you work for?" Jackson asked.

Frank hesitated for only an instant. "A few."

"He's lying," Jackson said, leaning back. "These are nothing but a couple of joyriding punks. I say we dump them."

"And I say you're not in charge here—I am," Ambler snarled.

"So far, I like you guys," Ambler told Joe and Frank amiably. "So now we move on to the second part of your test."

Frank watched as Ambler bent over and reached down between his legs to come up with a pair of Colt .45 automatic pistols. He balanced the guns in his meaty hands. "I guess you know how to use these," he said, holding them out to Frank and Joe.

Frank refused to take the gun. "I know how to use one," he drawled. "But I don't like to."

Ambler grinned. "You'll get over that," he said, dropping the guns into his lap. "If you're going to work with us, that is."

"Where you taking us?" Joe asked. "I don't like the country, guys. Crickets make me nervous."

"You want to join our business? Fine. We're going to see how you handle yourselves in a heist. Tell them about it, Jackson," Ambler said.

Jackson spoke to Frank and Joe without turning to them. "Okay, pay attention," he growled. "I don't want a pair of punks screwing us up."

"We'll take care of our end," Frank assured him.

Jackson grunted and continued. "We're paying a visit to a guy driving a new Mercedes-Benz 500 convertible out in Bernardsville—a superrich suburb. The car's a beaut—worth a fortune. The guy who owns it works in New York City, so he should be on the road sometime between five and eight A.M.''

"You guys really do your homework," Frank said.

"It helps things run smoothly," Ambler said coolly. "We wait outside the house. Once he hits the highway"—Ambler paused and grinned at Frank and Joe—"you two take his car."

He held out the guns to Frank and Joe. This time they had no choice but to take them.

This has been the worst night of my life, Joe said to himself hours later as he stared out the grimy window of the van, watching the sun rise. The brothers had spent the night squeezed in next to Jackson on a series of winding local roads. Finally the driver had stopped in the middle of nowhere for a few hours of sleep. But Joe found it hard to sleep with car thieves who snored.

Joe glanced at Frank, who was dozing lightly. It felt weird, Joe reflected, to wake up before his superactive brother. He checked out the van's mud-streaked windows once more and saw that they were parked on a beautiful, tree-lined country road. There were old stone walls beside the road. Behind the walls, hidden by trees, were mansions belonging to the wealthy.

Wealthy car drivers, Joe thought, remembering the conversation from the night before.

His thoughts were interrupted by the sound of an approaching car. Joe's heart leapt—he thought it was their quarry. Jackson woke instantly and peered out the window.

"It's Valdez," he said to Ambler, who had also been startled out of his sleep.

"Good." Ambler stretched, then turned back to Frank. "Wake up, sleepyhead," he joked, poking him in the side.

"I am awake," Frank said, snapping his eyes open. "What's up?"

"Our support car is here," Ambler said. "It's time to set the trap."

Five minutes later Joe found himself seated behind the wheel of the old Chevy, parked in a driveway on the same country road. The van was in another driveway about a quarter of a mile away with Valdez, Ambler, and Ambler's driver. Joe glanced over at Frank, who sat in the passenger seat beside him. The pair of Colt pistols lay between them.

"Nervous?" Jackson asked from the backseat. Joe peered into the rearview mirror and saw Jackson's sneering grin.

"Of course," Joe said. "If you're not on edge, you make mistakes."

"What do we do if we get separated from you or the van?" Frank asked. Joe could tell from the sound of his voice that Frank hated what they were doing as much as Joe did. They had no choice, though.

"That's simple—don't get separated," Jackson warned. "Don't let Ambler's nice-guy routine fool you. If he thinks you're stealing a car from him, he'll ice you—like that," he said, snapping his fingers.

Jackson leaned forward and patted Frank on the shoulder. "Don't sweat it. This will be a cinch. We follow the guy to the highway entrance ramp. The van nudges him—he slows down. You zip around in front, show him your guns, and order him out. Then you get in and follow us home. Just like we did with you."

Jackson stopped abruptly and looked up the road, suddenly alert. "Unless I'm mistaken, here's our boy now."

Joe felt icy panic grip his stomach as a new forest green Mercedes-Benz convertible approached. A moment later the Benz and van passed the Chevy.

"Let's move!" Jackson barked.

Joe started the Chevy and pulled out, following the van. His heart was pounding as they traveled along the tree-lined road. He could see, off in the distance, the entrance ramp to the expressway. He swallowed hard and gripped the steering wheel tighter.

"What's going on?" he heard Frank ask as the brake lights of the van blinked on.

"Don't panic." Jackson peered out the window. Joe saw the Benz pull into a convenience store parking lot, followed by the van. "He just wants to get a newspaper and coffee, I guess. Pull up next to him."

Joe pulled the Chevy into the lot between the Mercedes and the van. He glanced over at the middle-aged man in a business suit getting out of the Benz and trotting into the convenience store.

He left the engine running! Joe thought. Here was his chance to get the car—without flashing a gun. "Take the wheel," Joe barked to Frank.

In a flash Joe had leapt from the Chevy and was sprinting for the Benz. "Hey, come back here!" he heard Jackson shout.

Joe vaulted over the door and into the driver's seat of the idling convertible. He had depressed the clutch and was about to put it in gear, when Jackson appeared beside him at the passenger door. "What are you doing?" he screamed at Joe.

"Taking it—my way," Joe snarled. "Get in or get lost!" Jackson scrambled into the car as Joe peeled out.

"You're in a pile of trouble, hotshot," Jackson yelled as Joe guided the speeding car toward the entrance ramp of the highway. In the rearview mirror, Joe could see the Chevy and van following.

"The important thing is we got the car, right?" Joe said, pulling onto the entrance ramp.

At that instant Joe heard a siren's scream split the air. Looking in the rearview mirror, he saw a state police car pull out from behind some bushes next to the ramp.

Joe's heart flew into his throat. He was about to get caught speeding behind the wheel of a stolen car, with a loaded gun in his pocket!

Joe dropped into second gear. The powerful car roared onto the highway.

"Traffic is heavy," Joe barked at Jackson as

he sped onto the three-lane road. "I should be able to lose him."

"Watch it!" Jackson screamed as Joe darted in and out of traffic.

"Just shut up and enjoy the ride," Joe said. That state trooper was keeping up. By this time, Joe had the car in fourth gear. He glanced down at the speedometer. It was at one hundred miles per hour and creeping up—

"No!" Jackson screamed.

Joe looked up the road and gasped.

All three lanes of traffic were stopped less than two hundred yards ahead.

In seconds Joe's car would plow into a traffic jam at one hundred miles per hour!

Chapter

4

JOE REACTED without thinking.

He slammed on the brakes and grabbed the parking brake with his right hand. He jerked the brake up as he spun the steering wheel hard to the left.

The wheels of the speeding Benz locked and its rear end swung sharply to the right. Jackson's screams and the sound of squealing tires filled Joe's ears as the car skidded sideways down the road. Joe gripped the steering wheel, desperately trying to keep the car in a controlled skid.

As he struggled with the wheel, Joe darted a glance over his right shoulder. The rear of a truck, stalled in traffic dead ahead, was growing larger and larger. They were going to crash!

"Watch out!" Jackson screamed, ducking as

the Benz rushed up to the sharp metallic corner of the truck's rear bumper.

The Benz shuddered to a halt in a haze of smoke from burning rubber. Joe glanced over and saw that Jackson's door was barely touching the back of the truck.

"Better buckle up," Joe said as Jackson gazed at him, speechless with terror. Joe threw off the parking brake, fired up the stalled engine, and drove the Benz across the grassy median strip to the lanes heading in the opposite direction. He merged with the flow of traffic. Joe saw that the pursuing police car had been swallowed up by the traffic filling in behind it.

"We were lucky—real lucky," Jackson said, his voice husky with fear as Joe pulled the car into the right-hand lane. "Get off this road— now. The cops will be combing the county for us. We'll be lucky if we make it twenty miles without getting nailed."

Joe took the next exit onto a local road. From there they headed east, changing roads every few miles. Joe noticed that Jackson said little on the trip, except to give directions. The thief kept scanning the road behind them for police.

He's terrified, Joe thought. This guy is not nearly so tough as he wants me to believe.

As Joe headed east, the land became less rural and more urban. About an hour after they had left the highway, Jackson directed Joe onto another major road. Off in the distance, Joe could make out a city skyline.

"That's Newark, New Jersey," Jackson growled as they approached a large iron drawbridge. The city was now to their right.

"Get off at the last exit before the bridge," Jackson directed. Joe followed orders.

They were now on a four-lane road. To the right were the buildings of downtown Newark, to their left the oily waters of a large river. On the far side of the river were huge oil storage tanks.

"What is this, a port?" Joe asked. Jackson didn't answer, and Joe knew they must be getting close to the gang's headquarters. He remembered that the thieves could be shipping the cars overseas.

Joe eyed the row of large warehouses and wharves beside the road. The farther he drove, the more dilapidated the buildings became. A few of the buildings had been burned out, and most had boarded-up windows. An immense ship was docked at one of the wharves, confirming Joe's suspicion that the river was used as a deep-water port.

They approached a particularly shabby warehouse right on the river. "Turn in here and pull up to the main door," Jackson said.

Joe did as he was told. This must be the warehouse where the cars are shipped from, he thought. It had shattered windows, walls of rusty corrugated metal, and a roof of wooden planks filled with gaps. A strong breeze could take the place down in an instant.

As Joe pulled the nose of the Benz up to the main door, Jackson leaned over and pressed the horn two times, then two more. The door slid open.

Joe drove the car into the warehouse and was almost overpowered by the musty air and gasoline fumes. It took a moment for his eyes to adjust to the dim light filtering in through the rickety roof. The warehouse was empty except for a row of tarp-covered cars lined up along the right wall and a ratty sofa tucked into a corner. In the far wall was another huge door, which Joe realized must open onto the river.

There was a third, smaller door. It must lead to an office, Joe thought.

The huge door slid shut behind Joe. Joe killed the engine and turned around. He saw a large man in greasy coveralls standing with his hand on the warehouse door.

"Where's Ambler and the others?" the man asked.

"They're coming," Jackson said tersely. "I hope," he added under his breath. Joe's heart skipped a beat. He didn't want to think about what would happen if they didn't come back— or if the state cops realized that Ambler and Frank were in on the theft and arrested them. What would he do then?

Joe watched Jackson open his door and get out of the car. Jackson wobbled a bit, weak in the knees, Joe decided. Joe stepped from the car as the man in coveralls walked over and slid behind the steering wheel.

"Nice car," he said.

"It handles pretty well," Joe said nonchalantly. He stepped back as the man started the Benz and drove it across the warehouse, parking it beside the row of tarp-covered cars. Wishing he could get a look at the rest of the loot, Joe glanced over at Jackson.

"Stay here and keep your mouth shut until Ambler returns," Jackson commanded as the man in coveralls began covering the Benz with a tarp. "I have some phone calls to make." Jackson marched toward the office, entered it, and slammed the door behind him.

Frank Hardy fought the urge to press down on the gas and hurry the old Chevy down the road. He was in no position to get a speeding ticket. Besides, he had to stay behind the van if he wanted to find Joe.

Don't worry, Frank kept telling himself. Joe can look after himself. As Frank followed the van down a road that ran beside the river in Newark, he felt worried. He had no idea if Joe was alive or dead.

The van pulled up to an old warehouse that looked abandoned. He followed in the Chevy as Ambler and his driver honked the horn and stepped out of the van. As Frank got out of the Chevy, the warehouse door opened.

Joe was standing in the doorway. "What took you so long?" he asked.

"Joe!" Frank cried. "You're all right!"

"Sure," Joe said, maintaining his tough act. "Sorry about the tires on the Benz, Ambler. I took about an inch of rubber off them in that skid.''

Ambler chuckled. "You've got guts, kid."

"You call it guts, I call it stupidity," Jackson said, stepping out of the shadows.

"Get off my case, Jack," Joe said testily. "If I hadn't grabbed the Benz, we'd have tried stealing it on the entrance ramp—where the cops were waiting. We'd all be sitting in jail now.''

"You were lucky—this time," Jackson retorted. "The next time you ignore our plans and decide to play it solo, someone could end up dead.''

"Come on, guys," Ambler said. "Let's not fight. The important thing is we've got a full load for delivery. Everyone did their jobs, and now it's time to get paid.''

"How can we get paid?" Frank asked skeptically. "All the cars are right here. You haven't sold them yet.''

"You aren't used to a big-time operation," Ambler said to him. "J.R. sees that we're paid on delivery, with cash from previous shipments.''

"Ambler's right. This is a big operation," Joe muttered to Frank. "There must be twenty cars here.''

"The bigger it is, the more dangerous it is," Frank muttered back.

Minutes later the Hardys were sitting around an old card table outside the office door. Ambler was with them, holding a canvas bag. Jackson, Ambler's driver, Valdez, and the man in the coveralls sat at the table alongside the Hardys. Ambler reached into the bag and pulled out a huge wad of bills.

"Valdez, here's your cut," he said, counting out twenty hundreds.

Ambler then handed out equally large wads of cash to the man in the coveralls, Jackson, and his driver. Next he turned to the Hardys and smiled.

"And for our star pupils—" He peeled off five hundreds and dealt them to Frank, shoving the rest of the money into the bag.

"Hey," Joe said. "That's not fair. A chop shop would give us a lot more than that for a Benz."

"Yes, but would they offer you opportunity for advancement?" Ambler asked.

"What do you mean, 'advancement'?" Frank asked.

"You impressed me," Ambler said. "This is a big operation, boys. I need guys I can rely on."

Frank studied Ambler for a moment, pondering what to say. He knew that he and Joe could walk out right then with more than enough evidence to convict the people in that warehouse. Clearly, though, Ambler was only following orders from a higher-up—the mysterious J. R. Frank hated to drop out of the case without getting the head man.

Then, too, it was too big a risk to keep trying to fool these criminals, Frank decided. Just as he was opening his mouth to turn Ambler down, he heard Joe say, "Just give us the word, sir. We're ready."

Frank leaned back in his chair, stunned, as Ambler nodded and said, "Good. Come back here at midnight on Wednesday. Until then, lay low."

The fat man stood up and tucked the canvas bag under his arm. "That's all for now, gentlemen," he said. "Valdez, you stand guard till tonight. The ship sails with the loot at two. Jackson, meet me here at midnight.

"As for the rest of you—don't spend it all in one place!" Ambler said with a laugh.

"Interesting how you volunteered us both to help steal more cars on Wednesday," Frank said to his brother a short time later as the Hardys sat side by side in the old Chevy. Ambler had let them borrow the car until Wednesday, and Frank had parked it behind a dumpster about a quarter mile down the road from the old warehouse. From there they had watched as the other gang members, except Valdez, drove off.

"That's in two days, Frank," Joe reminded him. "Anything could happen by then. Meanwhile, we still have an inside view of an incredible smuggling operation."

"Do you really think Dad's going to let us come back here after the chase we gave him last night?" Frank demanded.

Joe shrugged. "We don't have to come back if we don't want to. Speaking of Dad, don't you think we'd better check in with him?"

"Definitely," Frank said. "He probably has the FBI out looking for us by now." He frowned. "It's a shame we can't bring him more information, though. Where those cars are being shipped to, for instance, and who J.R. is."

Joe nodded. Then he glanced at Frank. "I'll bet the answers to all our questions are right there in that warehouse office," he said, trying to speak casually. "It seems a shame to leave them there. What do you say?"

Frank tossed his brother a conspiring grin. "I say, let's find out more."

Silently the Hardys slipped out of the Chevy and hurried along the shoulder of the road to the warehouse. The warm noonday sun was causing Frank to break into a sweat. He glanced nervously up the road as they walked along, wishing it were night so they wouldn't be so exposed. At least he could take comfort from the fact that no cars or trucks had appeared on the road since they'd parked.

At the end of the driveway leading to Ambler's warehouse, Frank and Joe paused to stare at the derelict building. All was quiet.

"The coast is clear," Joe whispered. "Let's move."

The two Hardys scurried up to a corner of the warehouse. Frank peered through a dirt-caked window and saw Valdez stretched out on the shabby sofa in the far corner. Apparently he was asleep.

Frank followed his brother around the corner

of the warehouse. As they approached the rear of the building, Frank felt a cool breeze blow off the river. He peeked around the rear corner and saw a large loading dock abutting the warehouse. The loading dock—unlike the warehouse itself—was in good repair.

"That makes sense," Frank muttered to himself. "You can't load cars onto a freighter from a rotted dock."

"Psst, Frank!" Joe hissed. Frank saw that Joe had pried a piece of plywood from a boarded-up window on the side of the building. "The office is in here. Give me a boost." Seconds later Joe was scrambling over the sash and through the window.

"What do you see?" Frank whispered.

"These guys are total slobs," Joe replied. "Come look for yourself."

Frank stifled a cough as he climbed through the window into the dark, stuffy room. The floor was littered with old bottles, piles of papers, and stacks of yellowed newsprint. A tripod with a Polaroid camera stood in one corner. A safe stood in another, right next to a battered metal desk. But on top of the old desk, Frank noticed, was a new, well-cared-for fax machine and a sophisticated phone system.

"This must be how they receive their orders," Frank whispered, crossing to the fax.

"Frank, check this out," Joe whispered. He was standing in the darkest corner of the room next to a table. Frank saw four answering machines on the table, each plugged into a separate phone jack at the base of the wall. "What do you make of this?" he asked.

"I'm not sure," Frank said. "It looks like a monitoring system for phone taps. But why would car thieves be bugging phones?"

"We'll leave that for someone else to figure out," Joe said. "We need to find out where these cars are heading."

The boys returned to the desk. Frank opened a drawer and found a ledger and a set of neatly filed folders.

"This ledger shows all the cars stolen," he said, flipping through it. "See? Here's the last entry. It lists six cars—including the Benz you swiped this morning and the Porsche they stole from us last night."

"Does it say where they're going?" Joe asked.

"No," Frank said, disappointed. He opened one of the file folders, which contained sheets of fax paper. "Here are the orders Ambler was talking about," Frank said. Each sheet of paper was neatly typed and dated. Each one had cars listed, make and model number clearly indicated. "These people aren't kidding around," Frank said. "These order forms tell them exactly what to steal."

"Who are they from?" Joe asked.

Frank glanced to the top of the memo he held. "It reads, 'To: Ambler. From: Jolly Roger.' "

"Jolly Roger?" Joe said. "Wasn't that the name of the flag used by pirates in the Caribbean?"

"Yes," Frank said. "Jolly Roger also has the

initials *J.R.* Whoever is running this ring must have taken the name Jolly Roger as his alias.''

"He must think of himself as some kind of pirate," Joe said. "These sheets aren't much help. The fax number is blacked out so we can't trace them.''

"We'll take one, anyway," Frank said. "It has Ambler's name, and a list of stolen cars. At least this will link Ambler to the thefts.''

Frank took a sheet and carefully folded it and slipped it into his pocket. "Let's go before Valdez decides to come and straighten up in here.''

"Not likely," Joe said. A moment later he was back outside.

Frank and Joe sneaked through the shadows around the warehouse and headed back to the road.

"I'm hungry," Joe moaned as he and Frank walked in the blinding sunshine toward their car. "No dinner, last night, no breakfast today—I'm ready for lunch.''

"Me, too," Frank said. "But we've got to check in with Dad before we eat.''

"You're right," Joe agreed. "I wonder what he thinks happened to us?''

"I don't know, but—" Frank stopped short. "Uh-oh," he said, looking at the Chevy. "We may have trouble." Parked beside their car was a large van with a man leaning against it. He was tall and muscular and scowled as the Hardys approached.

"Do you recognize him?" Joe asked Frank out of the corner of his mouth.

"No," Frank replied. "But I doubt that he's in this neighborhood to sell Girl Scout cookies."

The man continued to scowl as the Hardys approached. "Hi," Frank said to the man when they reached their car. "Nice day, huh?"

The man didn't say a word. Glaring at the Hardys, he reached back and slid open the side door of the van.

"Get in," he growled. "Both of you—now."

Chapter

5

FRANK COULD TELL the guy meant business.

"Thanks, but we have a car," Frank said. "If you don't mind moving your van, we'll be on our way."

"Get into the van," the man repeated.

"Didn't you hear him, pal?" Joe's voice rose. "We have our own car. Besides, our father always told us never to accept rides from strangers."

"I think he'll make an exception this time," came a familiar voice from inside the van.

Fenton Hardy leaned out from the dark interior of the van and smiled at his sons.

"Dad!" Joe yelled. "What gives? Who is this clown?" Joe turned on the muscular man, his fists clenched.

"Relax, Joe," Fenton said. "I'm not a hostage. This is Agent Moorland of the FBI."

"The FBI?" Joe repeated. He turned to his brother. "You were right. He *did* call in the FBI to track us down!"

"No, I didn't." Fenton said with a chuckle. "After I lost your trail last night, I went to the New Jersey State Police. When I explained what we were working on, they put me in touch with the Newark branch of the FBI. It seems they've been trying to bust up the same car theft ring."

"Save the explanations for later," snapped Moorland, glancing warily in the direction of the warehouse. "Get in the van before someone sees us."

"Right." Fenton ushered his sons into the van. As he climbed in, Frank saw that the vehicle was customized for surveillance. Comfortable seats were placed in front of panels of electronic equipment—sound amps, video cameras, and other hi-tech detective apparatus. A petite and pretty blond woman in her midtwenties was sitting in one of the seats.

"Boys, meet Special Agent Skinner of the FBI," Fenton said, nodding at the woman.

"You're with the FBI?" Joe asked, obviously impressed. "I never met an FBI agent so,—er, so young."

Skinner's intelligent hazel eyes sized Joe up through a pair of round horn-rimmed glasses. "You must be Joe," she said, shaking his hand.

"Joe," Fenton said with a laugh, "your reputation precedes you."

Skinner turned to Moorland. "Impound that Chevy," she ordered. "Go over it for clues. I want it taken inside out before tonight. These boys may need it back by then."

"Got ya." As the man shoved the door closed, Frank heard the muffled sounds of the van's engine. Seconds later they were headed for downtown Newark.

"Congratulations, boys," Skinner said, giving Frank and Joe a smile. "You two have managed to do something we haven't—infiltrate Ambler's group."

"Yeah," Frank said. "He's even invited us to return when he gets his next set of orders."

"Good. When will that be?" Skinner asked, whipping out a small notebook and taking down notes.

"Wednesday," Frank said. "Here, we also took this from the warehouse." He removed the sheet of fax paper from his pocket and held it out to her. Skinner studied it briefly.

"Are there others like this?" she asked.

"Dozens," Joe said.

Skinner picked up a cellular phone and hit a speed dial button. "Lou?" she said into it. "Skinner here. I need a search warrant for a warehouse down on the riverfront. Have our legal department get right on it. We have material evidence giving us probable cause." She hung up and turned to the Hardys. "We'll raid the warehouse as soon as you two get back."

"Get back?" Frank turned to his father in surprise. "Where are we going?"

44

Skinner smiled at Frank. "That's what we need to find out," she said.

Thirty minutes later Frank and Joe were eating overstuffed hero sandwiches at the FBI's Newark office while Fenton Hardy and Agent Skinner waited impatiently for them to finish.

"This is your first big case, isn't it?" Frank asked in an effort to loosen the FBI agent up. When Skinner nodded grudgingly, Frank asked, "How long have you known about Ambler and his gang?"

"About six months," Skinner replied. Frank could tell that she knew she shouldn't discuss the case, but was dying to share her excitement with someone.

"Why haven't you nabbed him?" Joe asked through a mouthful of sandwich.

"Agent Skinner's after much bigger game," Fenton told him.

Embarrassed but pleased, Skinner explained to the boys, "Ambler is only a small part of a very large operation. There are hijacking rings just like his in Detroit, Chicago, L.A., and San Francisco. They all operate along the same lines."

"What happens to the cars after they're stolen?" Frank asked.

"We've traced some of them to developing countries," Skinner said. "Businessmen there can pay up to a hundred thousand dollars for stolen luxury and sports cars."

"That's a lot of money," Joe said and whistled.

"But less than it would cost if the cars were legally imported and taxes paid on them," Fenton pointed out. "That's what this case boils down to—someone acting as the middleman between hijackers like Ambler and the black markets in the developing countries."

Jolly Roger, Frank thought, remembering the name on the faxes.

"How does Ambler know where to find the exact cars he needs to fill his orders?" Joe asked.

"Good question," Skinner said. "The answer shows how sophisticated these crooks are. Shortly before Ambler started operating, there were a lot of petty burglaries in the prep shops used by luxury car dealers. You know what prep shops are, don't you?"

"Sure," Joe said. "Specialty shops where luxury cars are cleaned and polished before they're delivered to the new owners."

"Right," Skinner said. "When these places were robbed, the burglars didn't take much—but they left behind things of real value."

"Phone taps!" Frank said, remembering the answering machines he had seen in the warehouse.

"Exactly." Skinner beamed at him. "The burglars left bugs on the telephones in the prep shops. Every time the salespeople from the dealers called with orders for deliveries, they gave model numbers, addresses, everything. The hijackers were listening in. They'd wait for the model they needed, then grab it from the new owner."

"Fortunately," Fenton said, "no one has

been hurt in the hijackings so far. But that's bound to change. And that's why we have to help the FBI smash the operation."

"How?" Frank asked.

"Find out who the middle man is," Skinner said. "This fax you found is the first hard evidence we've had that there is a mastermind." She glanced down at the sheet of paper and laughed. " 'Jolly Roger,' huh? We think his center of operation is probably in the Caribbean, given where the cars have ended up. Once we find this J.R. and his records, we can root out the whole pirate operation."

"How can we help?" Joe asked.

"I want you on that ship Ambler told you about with that load of hot cars," Skinner said.

"There's just one problem," Frank said. "Why would Ambler send us along with the cars?"

Skinner took her notebook from her pocket. "Ambler's been sending Blue Jackson along to see that the cars are delivered. Then Jackson picks up the cash for them on the other end."

"Jackson—my old copilot," Joe said.

Frank nodded. "Ambler ordered him to meet him at the warehouse tonight."

"I doubt that he'll be there," Skinner said. "You two will take his place."

"How do we persuade Ambler to send us instead of Jackson?" Frank asked.

"Simple," Skinner said. "Just tell him Jackson tried to betray him today."

"What?" Joe asked, surprised.

"It's true—that state trooper you raced didn't

47

just happen to be waiting on that on-ramp," Fenton explained. "It was a setup. Jackson thinks someone is going to get killed. He doesn't want a murder rap hung on him. So Jackson went to his brother-in-law, who's a state trooper, and told him about the hijacking ring. They set up that trap."

"A trap that Jackson would manage to escape," Frank concluded.

Skinner smiled. "After you skipped, the trooper spilled the beans to his superiors."

"One thing's for sure," Fenton added. "Jackson won't be showing up tonight. We figure he's in hiding."

"Is that why you can't use him to help uncover J.R.?" Frank asked.

"It's one reason. We were going to search for him—until we learned you two were available. We trust the famous Hardys a lot more than a felon looking to cut a deal." Skinner looked directly into Frank's eyes. "So, what do you say? Will you help us smash these road pirates?"

Frank turned to his father. "What do you think, Dad?"

Fenton Hardy frowned. "It's a big risk. Of course, you'll stay in constant contact with us. If you get into trouble we'll be there." He sighed heavily. "In the end I guess it's your decision."

Frank turned to Joe. "How about you?"

Joe looked at his brother in amazement. "What do you think?" he demanded. "We're on our way!"

* * *

It was after midnight when Frank and Joe drove the old Chevy into the warehouse parking lot. "Ambler is here," Frank said, checking around the lot. The fat man's van was parked in a pool of light from an overhead spot.

"Whose car is that?" Joe asked. Parked beside the van was a new sports car.

"Only one way to find out," Frank said. "Let's go." They left the car and walked to the main door. "Here goes nothing," Frank muttered as he raised the main door of the warehouse.

As the door rattled open, three distant figures spun around to greet them. Frank saw light reflected off metal as the three pulled guns from their pockets. Frank shot his hands into the air.

"It's us!" he called. The men recognized the boys and relaxed, replacing their guns. Frank identified them as Ambler, Valdez, and—

Jackson! Frank realized. He and Joe exchanged a quick, surprised look. He must be planning to deliver the cars, take the money, and disappear. Shaken, Frank followed Joe into the warehouse.

"Hello, boys," Ambler said, his sharp eyes studying the Hardys with suspicion. "This is a pleasant surprise."

"What do you punks want?" Jackson snapped nervously.

"Surprised to see us, Jackson?" Joe remarked. Frank could tell by the bravado in his voice that Joe was winging it, not sure what to do about Jackson. "You can't be nearly as surprised as we are to see you—after what happened this morning."

"What happened this morning?" Ambler asked, tossing a glance at Jackson.

"Haven't you figured it out yet?" Joe asked. He glanced at Frank. Frank knew his brother was trying to decide whether to go ahead with the FBI's plan and betray Jackson to Ambler— even though Jackson was right there.

Frank thought about it—Jackson had returned to the warehouse at his own risk, and he clearly had no intention of turning Ambler in now. All he wanted was to disappear with Ambler's money. Frank gave a slight nod, and Joe continued, "Jackson set us up."

"He's lying!" Jackson barked, his voice cracking with fear.

"Hey, hey, relax." Ambler's sharp eyes cut from Jackson to the Hardys and back again. He tossed a beefy arm around Jackson's shoulder. Frank saw Valdez retreat cautiously into the shadows as Frank and Joe confronted the two road pirates. "I'm not going to do anything crazy," Ambler said to the quaking Jackson. "I just want to hear these boys out." He smiled coldly at Frank and Joe. "You have something to say?" he asked.

"He sold you out, Ambler," Frank declared. "Do you think it was just a coincidence that a state trooper was waiting right where Jackson had us grab that Benz?"

"And do you think it's a coincidence that the state trooper happens to be Jackson's brother-in-law?" Joe added.

"It's not true," Jackson protested. Ambler

quieted Jackson by wrapping his arm more tightly around his neck.

"Do you have proof?" Ambler asked Frank and Joe.

"Your only proof will be when Jackson runs off with your money," Joe said.

"How did you find this out?" Ambler asked.

"Let's just say we check out our partners better than you check out yours," Frank said cagily.

Ambler's fat face sank into a scowl. He tightened his grip around Jackson's neck, causing the younger man to squirm in panic. "I always knew you were a worm, Jackson," Ambler said. "Now I know you're a lying, back-stabbing worm!"

Still pinning Jackson by the neck, Ambler swung a beefy fist into his face. Frank's stomach knotted as the fist met Jackson's face. Jackson collapsed to his knees, blood streaming from his nose.

"That's enough," Frank said, stepping forward.

"I suppose you're right," Ambler said. "No sense in bloodying up my clothes." The fat man turned to Joe. "You don't like Jackson, do you? Not after he beaned you."

"As a matter of fact, I can't stand the guy," Joe said.

"Good," Ambler replied, and handed a large handgun to Joe. "Drag this worm out on the dock. And kill him."

Chapter
6

FRANK GLANCED at his brother, his heart pounding. The silence was broken only by Jackson's terrified whimpers. At last Joe reached for the gun.

"Time to take out the trash." Joe said as he hooked one of Jackson's arms and hauled the terrified man to his feet.

"Don't do it, Ambler," Jackson pleaded as Joe dragged him out the door to the loading dock. "These punks and not me? Ambler, listen to me!"

But Ambler had turned away. "Forget this unpleasantness," he told Frank. "Come check out what we'll be delivering." He led Frank to the cars lining the side wall of the warehouse.

An hour earlier the sight of half a dozen hot

cars would have fascinated Frank. Now, though, he paid no attention to the silver Maserati, the navy blue Jaguar, the black Ferrari Testarossa, or even the red Porsche. Frank strained his ears for anything to tell him how Joe had avoided his gruesome task.

It'll be all right, Frank told himself. Obviously Joe would never shoot anyone. Frank knew he would come back in a minute and say the gun is jammed. Or he would claim Jackson had overpowered him and managed to escape. Or that Jackson had dropped dead of a heart attack and Joe had tossed him into the river— *Blam!*

Moments before Frank heard the gunshot, Joe had walked Blue Jackson outside and propped the trembling man against a wooden piling facing the river.

"Hey, kid," Jackson pleaded, "you want money? I can get you money. Come in with me, and we can take over this whole operation—"

"Be quiet," Joe commanded. "Can you swim?"

"Can I swim?" Jackson asked, perplexed. Then his face cleared. "You mean, you're not going to kill me?" he mumbled.

"I'm no killer," Joe said with a scowl. "Listen to me, Jackson—you've got one more chance to straighten out your life. The FBI is on to you. If you so much as get a parking ticket, you've had it. But stay out of sight and out of trouble, and everything will be okay."

"Hey, I'll be a model citizen." Jackson held

up his right hand. "It's what I was planning anyway—"

"Knock it off," Joe said. He held the gun close enough to Jackson's face to keep him sweating. "When I fire this gun into the air, pretend it's an Olympic starter's pistol. Jump into the river and swim as though your life depended on it—because it does."

Jackson turned and faced the dark water of the river passing ten feet beneath them. He turned to Joe and managed a smile. "I don't know who you are, kid. But you're tougher than you look," he said.

"Yeah—and you're not," Joe said, raising the gun above his head and pulling the trigger.

Seconds later Joe strolled back into the warehouse from the darkened dock. He watched as Ambler turned and casually studied him. Frank was standing next to Ambler, his face ashen.

Joe presented the warm gun to Ambler. "The current is strong. I figure the body will make it out to sea."

"Good," Ambler said, handing the gun to Valdez. "Dispose of this," he said. While Ambler's back was turned, Joe winked at Frank and pointed his finger up, miming that he had fired the gun into the air. Frank nodded, relieved.

I knew Joe would find a way, he thought.

Ambler turned to the Hardys and favored them with an oily grin. "I'm very pleased, gentlemen," he said, rubbing his hands together. "Now I have a business proposition to discuss with you. How would you like to make a delivery for me?''

"Let me get this straight," Frank said after Ambler had made his offer. "You want us to oversee delivery of these cars, pick up the cash payment, and then stick around and spy on the person who hired you?"

"That's right," Ambler said. "I'm sick of working for chump change. All I get for each car is a lousy eight grand. I'll bet our friend J.R. sells them for ten times that."

"You don't know who J.R. is?" Frank asked.

"If I did, I'd have taken over by now, wouldn't I?" Ambler said testily. Then he caught himself, and his scowl melted into a warm smile. "But who better to change that situation than two pros like you? Jackson was so afraid of J.R., he refused to stay overnight at the drop-off point. I'd investigate myself, except—"

Except you're a total coward, Joe thought.

"Except my presence would arouse suspicion down there," Ambler concluded.

"If you've never met this J.R., how did you get involved in the pirate ring?" Frank asked.

"I was running one of the best chop shops in Newark," Ambler bragged. "About a year and a half ago, I got a call out of the blue. It was a man who said he had a business proposition for me."

"J.R.?" Joe asked.

"No," Ambler said. "I've never talked to him. Anyway, the man sketched out the workings of the pirate ring to me and, five days later, I got a package containing a fax machine, a phone bugging system—and twenty grand as a cash advance." Ambler grinned. "With twenty grand in my pocket, I decided to play along."

"And now you want to be a turncoat," Joe said.

"Well, why not?" Ambler said defensively. "We take all the risk. Why shouldn't we get all the gravy?"

"I hear you," Joe said with a glance at his brother. "Exactly what do you want us to do?"

"It's simple," Ambler said. "Deliver the cars and pick up the money. Normally, you'd leave immediately and go to the Cayman Islands to deposit the money in my bank account. This time I want you to look around, ask questions, and find out who J.R. is. We'll figure out where to go from there—together."

"Won't it look suspicious if we start nosing around?" Frank asked.

"It could," Ambler said. "You'll have to play it cool. You could 'accidentally' miss the flight to the Cayman Islands. There's only one flight from the drop-off point each week. That'll give you seven days to look around."

"One flight a week?" Frank asked, hardly believing his ears. "That's ridiculous."

"But true," Ambler said. "Fellows, you're heading off to beautiful Grand Key—home to the greatest smuggling operation since Blackbeard the Pirate's. I want that operation. Will you help me get it?"

Frank looked at Joe. Joe shrugged. "Okay,

Ambler," Frank said. "You've got yourself a pair of spies."

At that moment the sound of a faint whistle came through the open warehouse door. "Ah," Ambler said. "Your ship has come in."

Joe followed Frank and Ambler out of the warehouse and onto the dock. He saw a rusty old freighter pull up to the dock, its flat bow nestling against the loading dock. In the darkness Joe could barely make out crew members silently scrambling across the ship's deck to prepare the loading ramp that would be lowered. Then he heard a low rumble from within the warehouse. Joe saw through the open door that Valdez had uncovered all of the cars and started the engine of the first one.

"They'll have these cars loaded and hidden deep in the hold in twenty minutes," Ambler said. "We have to get you passports. J.R. sent us a handful of fakes. All we have to do is snap your photos and attach them. Come on," Ambler said. "We'll take care of it in the office. By the time the cars are loaded you'll be ready to go."

Half an hour later the Hardys emerged from the warehouse, clutching new, fake passports. As Ambler followed the brothers out the door to watch the last car being loaded, he said with a grin, "I guess you don't have your toothbrushes, either."

Joe watched as Ambler grabbed a duffel bag

from behind the door. "This is Jackson's stuff for the ship," he said. Ambler opened the bag and began pawing through it.

"Ha!" He laughed and took a book from the bag. "A Spanish phrase book. I guess he was planning to take a little trip at the end of his delivery."

"We told you he was selling you out," Joe said.

"He has enough clothes here to last for weeks," Ambler said, rifling through the bag. "They're about your size. You'll have to make do with these till you get to Grand Key."

"What if the crew asks us about Jackson?" Frank asked.

"If they do, you won't understand them," Ambler replied. "They're Greek—and no one but the captain speaks a word of English. If there's one thing you'll have plenty of, it's privacy."

An hour later Frank and Joe were standing on the deck of the ship as it steamed around Staten Island and into New York Harbor. A cool breeze ruffled Frank's hair as he took in the quiet, breathtaking scene.

Frank saw that they were alone on the water. At that hour there was no harbor traffic. Frank glanced off to his left at the beautiful, towering lights of the New York City skyline. He then peered straight ahead to the open dark sea.

And Grand Key, Frank thought. And their anonymous quarry, the mysterious J.R.

Joe interrupted Frank's thoughts.

"I can't get over how greedy Ambler is," Joe was saying. "Here he has a nearly perfect smuggling operation, and he wants to ruin it by trying to topple the big boss."

"It's funny," Frank said, watching the Statue of Liberty bathed in moonlight as they steamed past. "This is one case with two clients. The FBI—and a mobster."

Joe nodded. "Whoever J.R. is," he observed, "a lot of people want to see him finished."

Chapter

7

JOE WOKE EARLY on the morning of their third day at sea. As he had on the other two mornings, he went on deck to do a hundred push-ups and sit-ups in the open air.

The voyage had been smooth but boring, Joe thought as he worked out. He and Frank had spent the nights sleeping in a tiny cabin, which contained only a pair of ratty hammocks and a single porthole. They spent their days playing cards with a dog-eared pack they'd found in their cabin, or sitting on the deck watching the ocean waves.

If I never play Crazy Eights again, it'll be too soon, Joe thought, finishing the last of his push-ups.

Ambler had been right about the crew, Joe

mused as he rolled onto his back and began his sit-ups. The seamen had ignored the Hardys completely. Joe smiled as he recalled Frank's one conversation with the captain after their first meal. The old man had merely smiled at Frank.

"Ask no questions," he said in his heavily accented English, patting Frank's chest. "Tell no lies," he added, patting himself.

"Hope you've enjoyed your vacation," said a familiar voice. Joe stopped in the middle of a sit-up and peered over his shoulder. Frank stood next to the railing of the deck. "The captain came to our cabin after you left. We arrive soon. Are you ready?"

"Are you kidding " Joe said. He watched as they approached a small island. It had white sandy beaches crowned with a black, rocky ridge of volcanic stone. The rest of the island appeared to be covered with thick, lush vegetation.

"Your stop!" barked the captain from behind them.

"This is Grand Key?" Joe asked.

The captain shook his gray head. "Small Key," he said. "Your stop."

"It looks deserted," Joe observed. "You'd never imagine a smuggling operation here."

"No," Frank agreed. "Which means it's the perfect place to have one."

Frank and Joe stood beside the rail near the ship's bow as it sailed into the lagoon, the duffel bag at their feet.

"Where will we drop off the cars?" Frank wondered out loud.

"There," Joe said, pointing. "At the dock."

Frank strained his eyes. Although it was only a hundred yards away, Frank could barely make out a dock. It was painted to blend in with the white sand. A lone speedboat was moored to one end of the dock. Beyond the dock, partially hidden by thick vegetation, stood a large, camouflaged building.

"Someone must have dredged a channel right to the shore, so the ship could come in close," Frank said. Then he added, "Get ready. Someone's at the dock waiting for us."

The ship gently nudged the edge of the dock. Frank tossed their duffel bag over the railing as crew members threw thick lines over the pylons. As soon as the lines were secured, Frank climbed down a ladder to the dock, Joe close behind him.

A spindly man in a white shirt, khaki pants, and dark sunglasses greeted the Hardys as they stood on the dock. He's not exactly welcoming, Frank thought, noting the man's scowl.

"Where's Jackson?" the man demanded in a deep voice with a heavy Caribbean accent. As he spoke, a gold tooth flashed in the sun.

"He quit," Joe said. "Ambler made us the new couriers."

The man scowled at them for a moment. "That Ambler," he said at last, "he thinks he's a big man."

He marched off, leading the Hardys to the

warehouse. Behind them, the crew was lowering the ramp and preparing to unload the cars.

Frank carefully studied the warehouse as they approached it. The building was shaded by trees, its corrugated metal walls covered with vines. Frank shivered as they entered the warehouse— the interior was at least ten degrees cooler than it had been outside.

Frank glanced at the cracked and broken concrete floor, discolored by oil stains and covered with scattered piles of sand intended to absorb the spills. There were only two doors to the warehouse, Frank saw—the large loading bay they had entered and an old wooden door in the rear corner of the warehouse. Except for a huge, rusted gasoline tank on metal stilts against the right-hand wall and an old metal desk beside it, the warehouse was empty.

"Quite a setup you've got here," Joe said.

"Bootleggers built it during Prohibition, about seventy years ago," the thin man said. "It faces the sea, so they could smuggle liquor in and out and no one would know.'"

"I guess J.R. scouted out this place," Joe observed. "He certainly has things well in hand."

"Well enough to dislike unnecessary questions," the man said curtly. He threw a bulky manila envelope onto the desk. "This is all you ever need to know."

Frank stepped forward, opened the envelope, and took out five thick wads of dirty hundred dollar bills, all held together with rubber bands. Frank riffled through one of the wads. It held about one hundred bills. All told, there must be fifty grand here, Frank decided.

Frank looked at the man, who grinned broadly.

"Any more questions?" the man asked.

"I sure hate to see that baby go," Joe remarked as he and Frank stood on the dock and watched their Porsche disappear inside the warehouse.

"Look at it this way," Frank said in a low voice. "If all goes well, we're not losing a Porsche 911. We'll be gaining an entire luxury fleet."

The gold-toothed man jumped into the speedboat and gestured to the Hardys to join him. Frank and Joe strode down the dock.

"I will take you to Grand Key now," their pilot said as he fired up the engine. "While you are on the island, do not draw attention to yourselves. We want no trouble from the authorities."

"Don't worry about us." Frank dropped the duffel bag into the bottom of the boat. "We can look after ourselves." He hoped the FBI had a tail on them for backup—just in case they ran into trouble.

The man grunted in response. "When I drop you off at Grand Key," he said, "go to the immigration stand. Explain that you are tourists who came by water taxi. Do you understand?"

"I think we can handle that," Joe said.

"Take tomorrow's flight to the Cayman Islands," the man instructed. "It leaves at seven A.M."

Frank and Joe exchanged looks.

"Er—sure," Frank told the man. "But what if all the seats are already booked?"

The man stared angrily at Frank. "Don't miss that flight. That is my advice to you, if you wish to live a long and healthy life."

Their pilot was now steering the boat out of the lagoon and into the open sea. On the horizon Frank could see a chain of tiny islands—rock outcroppings similar in shape to Small Key. Frank decided to try getting more information on the islands from the gold-toothed man, in case they needed to return to Small Key.

"These are the Key Islands, right?" Frank asked, yelling over the roar of the boat's engine.

"Yes," the man said.

"Will it take long to get to Grand Key?"

The man shook his head. "Grand Key and Small Key are on opposite ends of the island chain, about seven miles apart. Far enough so that folks leave us alone."

Frank noticed that none of the islands were as big as Small Key, but some boasted scrub vegetation.

Frank peered over the windscreen of the boat. Looming ahead was Grand Key. Large enough for a small, pastel-colored town, the island also contained miles of spectacular white beaches.

"Vacationland, here we are!" Joe shouted. "Look—there's even a marina." Marina was a generous word for it, Frank realized, but the island did have a real man-made harbor with three large docks.

Frank glanced out toward the open sea and

saw a large pleasure boat chugging in toward the dock, long fishing poles sticking up from the deck. "Deep-sea fishermen," Joe said excitedly. Frank shook his head in amazement. It was almost impossible to imagine a big-time smuggler operating in this ocean paradise.

On the other hand, maybe it wasn't so hard, Frank thought as they drew closer to the island. The island seemed almost deserted. Except for the noise of their own motorboat, the place was as quiet as a ghost town.

"What's the name of this town?" Joe asked as their pilot pulled the speedboat up to the farthest dock.

"Georgetown," he replied curtly. "The immigration booth is at the end of the first dock. Go there immediately."

"I don't get it," Joe muttered to his brother as they walked along the deserted dock. "Where are the tourists? Where are the water skiers? Where are the girls?"

"It's like everyone was scared away," Frank agreed.

Frank peered down the single, unpaved road that ran from the dock, past a string of shops along the beach, and beyond. The first dozen or so buildings on both sides of the road were the traditional pastel-colored, wooden, two-storied structures that made Caribbean villages so attractive. But Frank noted that beyond these were several dozen one-story shacks built of unpainted cinderblock and covered with tin roofs. Apparently, life was not easy for all the residents of Grand Key.

Frank and Joe headed for the immigration booth, passing a few dusty jeeps and a couple of motorbikes propped up against nearby buildings.

"Rush hour on Grand Key," Joe remarked.

"You said it," Frank agreed uneasily. He approached a shack at the end of the first dock. The sign read Immigration and Naturalization. "Let's get officially greeted."

Inside the shack, a young man with chestnut-colored skin, wearing a dazzlingly white shirt and baggy shorts, sat with his feet propped up on a desk. An old magazine was spread out on his chest, and he was snoring.

"Good morning!" Frank called out. Instantly the young man snapped his eyes open wide and stared at the Hardys.

"And what do you want?" he asked in surprise.

"We just arrived by water taxi," Frank explained. "Is this where we have our passports stamped?"

Frank and Joe placed their fake passports on the desk, and the man carelessly flipped them open and stamped them. Then, without a word, he leaned back in his chair to resume his nap.

Bewildered, Frank and Joe took back their passports and left the office. "So much for law enforcement," Joe said, heading for the pastel buildings of the town.

"Fortunately, that's all the law enforcement we need," interrupted a cheerful voice with a broad British accent. Frank and Joe spun around to face a smiling, white-haired, deeply tanned old man standing behind them. He was carrying a long fishing rod in one hand and a box of tackle in the other. Frank guessed he was from the fishing boat that had just tied up near the end of the dock. The rest of the crew still seemed to be sifting through the day's catch.

"Welcome to the last unspoiled paradise in the Caribbean," the man said, dropping his tackle box and holding out his hand. "My name is Scobie, Reggie Scobie. I'm the chief of police on Grand Key. And who might you boys be?"

"My name is Goldstein, and this is Burnside," Frank said quickly, using the aliases on their forged passports. He shook the old man's hand. "We just got here from the Bahamas. We thought we'd try the fishing and windsurfing."

"Then you've come to the right place," Scobie said proudly. "There's plenty of both here, though none of that disco dancing and other rubbish. How long will you be with us?"

"Well," Joe said, "that depends on what we catch."

"And how much work I can get done here," Frank added impulsively. "I can run my business from anywhere, as long as I have access to a fax machine. Do you know if there are any on the island?"

"Fax machines?" Scobie's bushy white eyebrows shot up in surprise. "I shouldn't think so. Not much call for those here, you know. In fact, there are only three telephones on Grand

Key, last time I counted. One belongs to Jordan Reeves, our president. Another is in Mac Clarkston's office—he runs a fishing boat and is the man to see if it's fishing you want. Then of course, there's a phone at the Grand Hotel right down the road."

"Thanks for your help," Frank said, disappointed. "I guess I'll see if I can get by without one."

"Righto," the man said. Frank wondered if he was imagining the suspicious glint in the old man's eye. "Well, I must shove off for a conference with Reeves," Scobie added. "You gentlemen be sure to look me up if you need anything." As the brothers watched, Scobie threw his fishing gear into the back of one of the jeeps and drove off in a cloud of dust.

"Did you hear that?" Joe said as soon as he was gone. "The president of this one-dog island is named Jordan Reeves, whose initials would be J.R."

"That could be a coincidence," Frank said. "Let's not jump to any conclusions—we have plenty of time to investigate. Let's start by meeting the locals." He turned to face the main street in time to catch a woman peeking at them from a window above a grocery store. Farther down the road, a man walked out of a shop, stopped, and stared at the Hardys for an instant, then hopped on his motorbike and roared away.

"Good idea," Joe said. "While we're at it, let's try to buy some new clothes." He flexed his shoulders, constrained by Jackson's T-shirt.

"Good idea," Frank agreed. "These pants might come in handy in a flood, but till then I'd like some shorts."

As Frank and Joe walked down the main street, they encountered several townspeople standing on their porches or walking along the road. Each time, Frank and Joe offered a hearty greeting—but in every case the locals stared at them, surprised, and then looked away.

"This is weird," Joe said to his brother. "What do you think's going on?"

"Either J.R. has them all too scared to talk to strangers, or the place is under quarantine and nobody told us." Frank sighed. "This isn't going to make our investigation any easier."

"No kidding," Joe replied. "Hey, look—clean clothes!"

Frank checked out the display window of the tiny tourist shop nestled into the ground floor of a faded pink, two-story building. "Not that clean," he pointed out. Everything in the window, from seashell jewelry and brightly colored postcards to plastic palm trees and beach clothes, was covered by a thin film of dust. Obviously, the shop wasn't doing a thriving business.

A young boy around ten years old sat leaning against the wall on the front porch. The Hardys grinned at him as they made their way inside. The boy only studied them in silence.

Inside, Joe spied a tank top displayed in the middle of the store. "Cool," he said, moving closer to inspect it. As he did so, he brushed the duffel bag against a pyramid display of suntan-oil bottles, sending them crashing to the floor.

"What's going on out there " came a woman's voice from the back of the store.

"Sorry," Joe called, putting down the duffel bag. "We had a little accident. I'll clean it up."

"I'll help," Frank said, setting down the yellow cash envelope on a nearby chair and joining his brother on the floor.

"Ah, don't worry about it," came the voice, much closer now. Frank looked up and saw a large woman walking in from the back of the store. "I have to tell you, it's a pleasure having customers in here, no matter what you—" Frank saw the smile fade from her face as she noticed something behind them. "You!" she snapped in anger. "Put that back! Now!"

Frank turned and saw a rush of movement out the front door.

Then he looked at the chair where he had left the envelope full of cash.

The envelope was gone!

Chapter

8

"THE MONEY!" Frank cried.

Joe turned in time to see Frank rush out into the blinding sunshine. Scrambling to his feet, Joe followed. He saw Frank in hot pursuit of the boy who had been leaning against the storefront.

"I'll head him off!" Joe yelled as the boy sprinted toward a motor scooter parked across the street. Joe angled off in the direction he thought the scooter would take just as the boy kick-started the engine.

The scooter shot off just in front of Frank's grasp. With a broad smile on his face, the boy watched Frank stumble to a stop. The thief didn't see Joe until he had grabbed the boy around the waist. The two of them tumbled to the dusty road as the scooter crashed into a pile of baskets.

"Gotcha!" Joe pinned the boy to the dirt. He struggled in Joe's grasp as Frank ran up to them.

"Let him up, Joe," Frank said. Frank glared at the boy as he got to his feet, brushing dust off his shorts with his free hand. "All right," Frank snapped. "Hand it over."

"Hand what over, man?" the young boy asked, innocence filling his handsome features.

"You know what," Joe snapped.

"Oh," the boy said, pulling the envelope from inside his shirt. "I thought someone forgot to mail it. I was going to drop it in the post."

"Liar," Joe said, taking the kid's arm.

The boy's eyes grew twice as large and round. To the Hardys' surprise, his face crumpled up and he began to wail.

"Malcolm Bradbury," snapped a woman from behind them, "you're going to get into a heap of trouble." Joe turned to see the shopkeeper standing in the doorway of her store. When Joe let go of the boy, he instantly stopped crying.

"Don't worry about me, Miss Thompson," Malcolm called good-naturedly, wiping the tears from his face. "I can watch after myself." As the woman sighed and returned to her store, the pint-size thief gave Frank a look of triumph.

"What other kinds of trouble do you get into?" Frank asked.

"None," Malcolm said saucily. "Someone leaves something lying around, I pick it up. No trouble." Joe shook his head in disbelief.

"Good morning to you, Malcolm," called an old man as he emerged from a nearby fruit stand.

"Good morning, Mr. Bending," Malcolm said, as he picked up his motor scooter. "How is Ginger?"

"Just fine, thank you for asking. Here—you might as well have this." The old man tossed an orange to Malcolm. When he noticed Frank and Joe, the smile vanished from his face. He turned away quickly as two other islanders went by on bicycles, greeting Malcolm as he wandered back to his scooter.

"This kid must be the most popular thief on the island," Joe muttered to his brother. "Everyone seems to know him."

"That's just what I was thinking," Frank replied. "Maybe we could ask him a few questions about this place—like why he's practically the only person who'll talk to us."

"What?" Joe asked in disbelief. "Is the sun getting to you already, Frank? This kid just tried to lift fifty grand off us."

"That doesn't mean we can't talk to him," Frank said.

"That's what you say," Joe remarked. "This Malcolm can't be trusted."

"Hey," Malcolm said, wheeling his motorbike over to the Hardys. "I heard my name. What do you people need? You want to hire a guide?"

"A guide?" Frank laughed. "For what? This town's only about ten blocks long."

"But there's plenty of things going on all over

this island," the boy said eagerly. Joe marveled at how quickly he seemed to have changed roles. "You want to sail, I can find a boat for you. You want to fish, same thing. But I have a feeling you guys are here to work," he added, his eyes narrowing shrewdly.

Joe flushed. "What makes you say th-that?" he stammered. "We're just tourists, that's all."

"No, I don't think so. Tourists don't come here much anymore." Malcolm eyed each brother thoughtfully. "But I don't care what you're up to," he added with a sudden grin. "Pay me and I'll take you anywhere. No one knows this island better than me."

Frank threw his brother a questioning glance, and Joe shrugged in exaggerated resignation. "Okay," Frank said to Malcolm. "I'm Frank, he's Joe, and we'll pay you ten dollars a day to take us wherever we tell you to."

"Twenty," Malcolm promptly responded.

"Fifteen," Joe countered sternly. "That's our last offer."

Malcolm smiled. "Throw in meals, and you two have found the last guide you'll ever need," he said.

"The first place we want you to show us is where we can stay," Frank said twenty minutes later. The Hardys and Malcolm had returned to the store, where Frank and Joe bought fresh clothes and arranged to rent a pair of motor scooters for their stay on the island. They were now mounting their scooters outside the storefront.

"Simple," Malcolm said. "There is only the Grand Hotel. Follow me." He started his scooter.

The boys were surprised when they drove only four buildings down the road before stopping in front of a large, yellow, three-story edifice with the words Grand Hotel painted in fading black letters over the front door.

"Whew—some trip. I'm exhausted," Joe quipped as they followed Malcolm inside. Joe noted with pleasure the wicker chairs and card tables on the open front porch, and the polished teak paneling inside. Clearly, he thought as he glanced into a large dining room to the left of the lobby, the Grand Hotel was once host to a major holiday crowd.

"This way," Malcolm commanded, as he led them across the spacious lobby. A large ceiling fan hung from the center of the room, keeping the vast space cool. Off to one side, a broad staircase led to the upper floors. A handsome teak check-in desk commanded the center of the room. Behind it was an interior office.

Malcolm strode confidently up to the desk and banged a bell on the counter. The Hardys followed.

"Welcome," a silvery voice called out from the office behind the desk. Joe peered into the dim room and smiled, very impressed. Walking out to greet them, a warm, welcoming smile on her face, was one of the most beautiful women Joe had ever seen.

"Hello there, Malcolm," the woman said in a charming British accent. Joe realized, now that she stood in the light, that the woman was some-where in her late thirties or early forties. Her deep tan and honey-colored hair streaked pale by the sun made her look like a teenager from a distance.

"How do you do?" she said to Joe, holding out a slender hand. "I'm Miranda Watt, owner of this establishment. I take it you're our guests?"

"We'd like to be, Miss Watt," Joe said.

"Call me Miranda, please."

"Okay, Miranda," Frank said. With a grin, he took her hand himself and gave it a hearty shake. "My name is Frank Goldstein, and this is my friend Joe Burnside. We'd like a room for the night—maybe longer if we're lucky."

"Wonderful." Miranda offered him a brilliant smile. "I'm afraid we aren't quite a four-star es-tablishment, but we do have clean rooms and affordable prices." She started to slide the regis-tration book across to the Hardys when her hands froze midway.

"I'm sorry," she said haltingly. "Did you say—maybe longer?"

"We hope so," Joe said, taking the book and signing his alias on one of the lines. "We've come here for the water sports."

"Really? And—how did you hear about this place?" Her smile had faded completely by now.

Joe glanced at Frank, wondering if he found Miranda Watt's behavior odd, too. It was almost as though the hotel keeper didn't want them as guests!

"A friend of my father's told me about it,"

Frank said to her. Joe could tell from Frank's voice that he was curious too. "He said that in the old days this was a great place to kick back and relax."

"In the old days, yes," Miranda said with a sigh. She seemed to have recovered somewhat, Joe noticed. "That was when my husband was alive. He built this hotel back in the sixties. Unfortunately, Grand Key seems to have passed out of fashion."

She watched Frank sign the register, then added sharply, "You do know there's only one flight each week off the island, don't you?"

"The next one's tomorrow morning," Joe told her. "That's why we thought we'd stay awhile. A week's plenty of time to find out if Frank's father's friend was right."

"Hmm. Well, I'm sure you'll have a marvelous time," Miranda said blandly. "The fishing here is the best in the region, and the diving and windsailing are excellent. I'll put you two in Room 207," she added, writing their room assignment in the registration book.

"Don't we get keys?" Joe asked as Miranda closed the book.

"Good heavens, no," she said with a laugh. "None of our rooms have locks. There's no crime on Grand Key."

"None?" Frank asked, turning to Malcolm, who smiled innocently.

"Will you be checking any valuables?" Watt asked Joe. Joe considered giving her his envelope, but decided it would be safer where they could get to it.

Frank answered for him. "No, thanks. But there is something I'll need if we stay here all week."

"What's that?" she asked with a smile.

"A fax machine," Frank said. "I can't stay out of touch with my business for long."

Miranda stared at Frank for a second, then threw back her head and laughed.

"Excuse me for laughing," she said, "but I'm afraid you'll be quite out of touch here. We have no fax machines, no television—nothing from the modern world that could disturb our peace." Miranda smiled at Frank. "I'll tell you a secret, though," she said, leaning toward him. "I smuggled a computer in for my business several years ago. But for heaven's sake, don't let my neighbors know!"

"All right," Joe said as he opened the door to their room minutes later. "A real bed!"

He flopped onto one of the twin beds. Frank stood in the doorway of the airy, wallpapered room.

"All I need now is lunch," Joe said, "and I'll be a happy camper."

"Grand Hotel serves the best food in town," Malcolm told them. "And you owe me lunch."

"You guys go ahead," Frank said. "I'll be down in a minute."

As Malcolm and Joe left the pleasant room, Frank scanned the ceiling. A large half-globe of frosted glass hung by chains from the ceiling, serving as a cover for the light bulb there. Frank stood on a chair and stretched up, depositing the envelope in the globe. It made a faint shadow against the glass, but not enough that anyone would notice, he decided.

Malcolm was waiting for Frank at the foot of the lobby staircase.

"Hurry, man," he said. "My belly is growling."

Frank saw Joe at the opposite side of the lobby, reading a bulletin board located beside the front door.

"Check it out," Joe muttered, nodding excitedly at the bulletin board.

"Mac Clarkston," the notice read. "Fishing Parties, Deep-Sea Fishing, and Other Boating Excursions." A waterfront address was printed below it, along with a fax number.

"Forget him, man," Malcolm chided, noticing what Frank was looking at. "You want to fish? I have an uncle who will take you out. He knows all the best places, and will charge less than Clarkston—"

"Does your uncle have a fax machine?" Joe asked impatiently.

"What?" Malcolm said, eyeing him. "You want to send a message to the fish before you catch them?"

They had only arrived a couple of hours earlier, and already Frank sensed an interesting lead taking shape. "I think we'll visit Mr. Clarkston this afternoon," he said, giving Joe a nod.

As the three of them entered the dining room,

Frank admired the high ceiling and enormous French doors opening onto a porch. About a dozen round tables covered with white tablecloths were scattered around the room.

"Not bad," Joe remarked. The room was empty except for one table in a shady corner. Sitting there were Grand Key's police chief, Reggie Scobie, and another older man in a dark business suit. The men were surrounded by stacks of papers and seemed deep in conversation.

"Hello again. How do you like your room?" asked a pleasant feminine voice. Frank turned to see Miranda Watt standing behind them, menus in hand.

"Just fine," Joe said, returning her smile. "Now we're ready to try out the dining room."

She led them to a table in the center of the room. Scobie smiled and waved at the Hardys. As the other man scowled at them suspiciously, Frank wondered if he was President Reeves.

"We're a little shorthanded here, so I'm playing hostess for the time being," Miranda explained apologetically. "Waitress and cook, too, I'm afraid."

"Can I have hot dogs?" Malcolm asked.

"No problem," Miranda replied, ruffling his hair. "And how about you fellows?"

"What seafood do you recommend?" asked Joe.

"I can make you an excellent conch salad," Miranda said.

"Sounds good," Joe said.

"Make it two," Frank added.

Miranda headed for the kitchen. Frank peered over at Chief Scobie's table.

"Who is that with Scobie?" Frank asked Malcolm.

"Jordan Reeves," Malcolm said. "He's been president of Grand Key for ten years—ever since we became independent from Great Britain."

Frank nodded, his suspicions confirmed. He remembered Scobie's mentioning that Grand Key's president owned one of the island's three telephones. "Does he do a good job?" Frank asked.

"Yeah," Joe added, suddenly curious. "It seems to me this place could use more tourists."

"Mr. Reeves hates tourists messing up his pretty island," Malcolm said with a snort. "The rest of us can starve, trying to live off the sale of the fish we can catch, what does he care? He lives off a trust fund. It doesn't matter to him if the airplane never brings people to Grand Key." Malcolm's eyes narrowed with suspicion. "But why do you want to know all this?" he asked the Hardys.

"We're good tourists," Frank said, mimicking Malcolm's earlier innocent look. "We like to know what's happening where we hang out."

"And I say if you're tourists, I'm a New Yorker," Malcolm retorted easily. "Listen to me. I've been a guide for people here since I was seven. And nobody's ever asked me about the president before."

"Okay, forget it," Frank said, fearful of blowing their cover. "Ah! The food!" he added with relief. Miranda was returning with two bowls piled high with leafy greens, chopped, luscious vegetables, and colorful bits of conch spread on top. As she approached them, Frank risked a quick glance at President Reeves. So the president lived off a trust fund, he reflected. And he hated tourists? The person on the island most likely to resent intruders would certainly be J.R. Frank wondered what the chances were that the scowling man arguing with Police Chief Scobie could be living off the proceeds from several hundred stolen automobiles.

"Here you go," Miranda said, setting the bowls in front of Frank and Joe. "Malcolm, I'll be right back with your hot dogs."

"I hope so," he grumbled. "I'm hungry."

Miranda turned toward the kitchen, but before she could go, Joe impulsively grabbed her by the arm.

"Excuse me, Miranda," Joe said with a glance at his brother. Frank knew the glance meant that Joe didn't want to waste time being cautious.

"Yes, Joe?" she asked, a faint smile on her lips.

"Uh—well, I was wondering. We're new here, and maybe we're just over-curious—"

"Yes?" Miranda glanced from Joe to Malcolm, her smile freezing.

"Being out of fashion is one thing," Joe blurted out. "But, Miranda, this is different. Grand Key is empty!"

Miranda pulled back. She seemed offended, Frank noted. "You may consider it empty," she

said with dignity. "Here, we call it perfect."
With that, she disappeared into the kitchen.

"Talk about hot and cold," Frank said, returning to his seat and facing Joe. "First she complains because there aren't any vacationers. Then she gets offended because you ask her why."

"Of course she gets offended, man," Malcolm said angrily as Joe dug into his salad. "Put yourself in her place. How would you like to try to run this hotel, pretending everything was fine when all the time your rooms were empty and your kitchen was bare? Besides, do you expect her to complain when the cause of the problem is sitting right over there?"

Frank looked at Malcolm in surprise. "You sure do talk old for your age," he remarked. "If I didn't know better, I'd—" Frank stopped short. His mouth fell open in shock as he glanced at his brother. Joe froze, a fork filled with the salad halfway to his mouth.

"What is it?" Joe asked, squirming slightly as something light and feathery tickled the side of his arm.

"Don't move, Joe," Frank said in a low voice, slowly rising to his feet.

Frank's eyes were fixed on the four-inch-long scorpion scurrying from the forkful of salad up Joe's bare arm.

Chapter

9

"WHAT IS IT?" Joe hissed, feeling the feathery tickle on his forearm. His arm ached from tensing his muscles. As he peered down, he saw the segmented body of the venomous scorpion scuttle onto the top of his arm. "Get rid of it."

"Don't move," Frank said, his fingers clutching at a knife. Frank leaned over the table and held the knife forward. He stopped about six inches from Frank's arm. The scorpion stopped moving.

Suddenly the scorpion lashed its tail, the poison stinger poised ready to plunge into Joe's arm!

Frank's knife flashed. In one fluid move he slipped it under the scorpion and flicked the creature into the air. It came to a halt on the floor about ten feet away, where Frank crushed it beneath the heel of his shoe.

Frank examined the squashed scorpion, then turned to his brother and smiled. President Reeves and Police Chief Scobie broke out in applause.

"What's going on?" Miranda Watt appeared in the doorway, holding a plate of hot dogs and french fries.

Malcolm turned to her. "You didn't rinse the lettuce," he said matter-of-factly. "Is that my lunch?"

"Oh, my goodness." Miranda crossed to the table, shock on her face. "Was that a—?"

"A scorpion," Joe said, rubbing his forearm. "I almost ate a scorpion."

"I'm so sorry," Miranda gasped. "It must have gotten into the pantry somehow."

"We have a problem with venomous creatures on our island," boomed a deep voice. Frank raised his eyes to see Jordan Reeves standing beside their table, a hard expression on his face. Scobie stood beside him.

"That's true. Our last fatality was due to a scorpion sting," Scobie recalled philosophically. "It happened about six months ago. A young tourist put on his shoes after a swim at the beach—one of the little beasties had crawled into the shoe while he had been swimming." The old man snapped his fingers. "Killed him like that, poor devil."

"All visitors are wise to watch their step," Reeves said ominously.

*   *   *

"Are you sure he was threatening you?" Agent Skinner asked incredulously.

It was thirty minutes later, and Frank was sitting in an old wooden phone booth in the rear of the hotel lobby. Once the boys had changed into their new clothes, Frank had left Joe and Malcolm and gone to check in with Skinner and their father.

Frank reached Skinner at her Newark office. After she explained the FBI hadn't been able to tail them, Frank told her where they were, and related the incident with the scorpion. He also told her about Jordan Reeves's personal income and his odd reaction to Joe's near-miss.

"We've hardly had a warm welcome to the island," Frank said. "And if Malcolm is right about Reeves's intentionally keeping tourists out, he could be the boss of the car piracy ring."

"Hmmm," Skinner said. "If Reeves is involved, it makes for a very delicate diplomatic situation."

"So what should we do?" Frank asked.

"I'll be there in thirty-six hours," Skinner decided. "In the meantime, keep your eyes and ears open. Don't get on that plane tomorrow morning."

"Right," Frank said.

"And be careful," Skinner said. "We want to bust J.R., but we don't want you dead."

"I'm touched by your concern," Frank said wryly.

Frank hung up the phone and crossed the

lobby to go outside where Joe and Malcolm sat in the sweltering sunshine.

"What's the scoop?" Joe asked his brother.

"Everything's A-okay at home," Frank said cryptically. "In fact, a friend of ours might join us soon."

"A friend?" Joe asked.

"Yeah, our pretty, ambitious friend," Frank said significantly.

"Good," Joe said with enthusiasm. "I just hope we have something to show her by then."

"Enough jabbering," Malcolm said with a grin. "Are you gentlemen going to sit around all day, or do you want to have some fun?"

"Have some fun," Frank said with a glance at Joe. "We can start with some deep-sea fishing."

In spite of Malcolm's insistence that his uncle was the better fisherman, Frank and Joe insisted on trying Mac Clarkston.

"You see?" the boy said, when they arrived outside a large, unpainted shanty on the water. A private pier branched from one side out into the ocean. The words Mac Clarkston Fishing Parties were painted in fading green letters on the side of the shack facing the road. "He's not even home."

Joe studied the shack. Unlike the other buildings on Grand Key, this one had a phone line running from the roof to the main road. Joe peered through one of the windows into Clarkston's living room. The furnishings were sparse: a pine table and two chairs, an overstuffed sofa, a low dresser, and a roll-top desk. Joe squinted at the desk.

"Faxes," he murmured. There on the desk were the telltale papers curled up into tight cylinders. Joe stood on tiptoe, trying to read the top of the nearest—

"Ahoy, there!"

Frank and Joe stepped back from the shack. A large fishing boat was chugging up alongside the pier. Joe saw a beefy, broad-shouldered man in his late sixties or early seventies at its helm. The man had a heavy black beard specked with gray and skin almost as black as his beard. He was watching the Hardys suspiciously. "Can I help you?" he called.

"Mac Clarkston?" Joe yelled.

"The same," the man responded.

"We're interested in going fishing," Joe said.

"Always happy to oblige." Clarkston tossed a line over a pylon on the dock. He nodded at Malcolm, then asked the Hardys, "When were you thinking of going?"

"How about this afternoon?" Frank asked.

Clarkston looked at him in genuine surprise. "You boys *do* need a fishing guide. The best you can hope to catch at this hour is a sunburn." He stepped onto the dock, a large spear gun in his left hand.

"When do you recommend we go?" Joe asked, studying the man curiously.

"Tell you what," Clarkston said. "Show up here tomorrow morning at four-thirty. I guarantee you'll catch something worthwhile."

"It's a date," Frank said. "In the meantime,

maybe you could give us a water tour of the islands.''

"Sorry. No can do," Clarkston said gruffly, striding to the door of his shack. He set the spear gun against the wall, removed a large ring of keys from his pocket, and found one to unlock his door. "I have paperwork to get to. I'll see you boys tomorrow at dawn." He opened his door, entered the shack, and slammed the boys out.

"The guy's a fisherman," Frank said skeptically as he walked with Joe and Malcolm back to their scooters. "What paperwork could he have?"

"Mr. Clarkston's always busy with paperwork," Malcolm said importantly. "Miss Thompson says he's practically a hermit, making women like her lonely."

Joe chuckled as he watched Clarkston pull the shades down over his windows. "I definitely saw some faxes in there," he said. What he didn't add, with Malcolm listening, was that he planned to get inside to read them.

"What is it with you and fax machines?" Malcolm asked.

"Well, it looks like fishing is out," Joe said, ignoring his question. "What do you suggest we do with the rest of the day?"

Malcolm held his finger up in the air. "The breeze is up," he declared. "Let's windsurf."

Twenty minutes later Frank and Joe had changed into their swimming trunks and were sitting on the beach near the Grand Hotel. It was a perfect Caribbean day—turquoise waves crashed against the white sand while Malcolm went off to rent windsurfing boards. The Hardys grabbed the opportunity to talk about what they'd learned so far.

"Let's lay it out simply," Frank said, tracing a design in the sand. "I guess our prime suspect is Jordan Reeves, even if he is president of this place. He has the right initials. He has money. His attitude stinks."

"What about Mac Clarkston?" Joe protested. "He has a boat and a fax machine, lives like a hermit, and I didn't think his attitude was so hot, either."

"Nobody's been friendly," Frank admitted with a laugh. "Maybe it's something in the water."

"Except for Miranda Watts," Joe pointed out. "She's been friendly. I mean, except for letting that scorpion get into my lunch—"

At that both boys burst out laughing. "So they're a strange bunch," Frank said. "We still have a job to do. Tomorrow morning Malcolm and I will go fishing with Clarkston and tell him you decided to sleep in. That will give you a chance to nose around his place for clues."

"Excellent," Joe said, rubbing his hands.

"In the meantime," Frank added, "we need to investigate Reeves." He stopped abruptly as Malcolm came trotting to them from across the beach.

"It's all set," Malcolm announced proudly. "Let's pick up our boards."

"Okay." Joe stood up. "Where should we go to surf? The president's palace?"

Malcolm grinned at him. "You're kidding, man. There's nothing to see."

"No, we're serious," Frank said. "We'd like to check out Reeves's place. Say we saw the president's palace."

Malcolm shrugged. "Suit yourself," he said. "You could probably even walk in and look around."

Minutes later the Hardys and Malcolm were skimming the turquoise waves on windsurfing boards, heading for the presidential palace.

"This is my kind of job," Joe called to Frank, as they made their way across the sun-dappled water. Frank agreed. He felt light-years away from the grimy warehouse, fat Ambler, and the stolen cars.

"There it is," Malcolm called, pointing to a building on shore. They all stopped, letting their sails drop into the water. Frank straddled his board, dangling his legs in the warm water. Joe and Malcolm jumped into the water, pushing their wind surfers toward Frank.

"Wow. That's hardly a palace," Frank said. The residence was a fairly small cinderblock building with a tar paper roof. Phone wires fed into a telephone pole beside it. A simple dock led from a small beach at the water's edge right up to a picture window at the back of the building.

"I told you," Malcolm reminded him.

"But you said he was rich," Joe protested.

"Sure. But he's not a big spender," Malcolm said.

"You said it would be all right if we looked around?" Frank asked hopefully.

"I said he wouldn't be here. You'd better hurry," Malcolm added. "He could turn up any minute now."

The Hardys paddled quickly to shore. Malcolm remained on lookout in the water.

"It's not bad inside," Frank said to his brother, standing in the center of the living room, checking out the comfortable furnishings of a well-to-do, middle-aged bachelor. Reeves seemed to have a fondness for antiques, Frank noted. Polished side tables, sofas, and hassocks cluttered the room. The walls were covered with framed black-and-white photographs and certificates honoring the president.

"No fax machine here," he heard Joe mutter. "The most modern thing is the electric lamp."

"He wouldn't necessarily keep any pirating equipment in full view," Frank admonished him. "Let's try the bedroom."

Frank headed down a narrow corridor leading to the back of the house. To the left, past a dining room, bathroom, and kitchen, was a large bedroom with a view of the ocean.

"Nothing here, either," he said to Joe, who had followed him to the room. "Maybe there's an office behind the kitchen somewhere." Just then he heard a long, high whistle from outside.

'It's Malcolm," Joe said. "Reeves must be coming."

The brothers quickly slipped out of the house.

Malcolm was pointing to a speedboat skimming over the water toward the house.

Hunching over to avoid being seen, Frank and Joe ran to their boards and hurriedly paddled out to join Malcolm. "Let's dive till the boat passes," Frank said nervously. "I don't want anyone to know we've been nosing around."

"Okay," Joe agreed. "What do we do with our boards?"

Malcolm shook his head in amusement. "There's not a strong tide. They'll stay close. We're right next to a coral reef, it should be fun to dive here." The boy slipped under the water.

Frank filled his lungs with air and slid into the warm water below, too.

The temperature is perfect, Frank thought as he kicked under the surface, following Malcolm and Joe to a brilliant coral reef about ten yards ahead of them. Sunlight filtered down through the water, so clear that Frank could see schools of colorful tropical fish darting in and out of the reef. As he dove, he wondered about Reeves. Was there a hidden room in the back of his house where he conducted his business? I might never know, Frank realized, if I don't think of a way to get back in there.

Malcolm, obviously familiar with the reef and used to long dives, disappeared into a deep crevice in the reef. Joe followed close behind. Frank paused, hearing Reeves's boat pass by.

Kicking hard, Frank shot to the surface. He wiped the water from his eyes in time to see

Reeves dock his boat. As he tied up, Reeves turned back in Frank's direction.

Frank took a deep breath and dove back underwater. He swam down, looking for Malcolm and Joe.

Just wait here, he told himself, treading water to stay in place. They'll show up. Impatiently, he waited.

After a few seconds Frank began to get worried. His lungs had begun to ache. Maybe Malcolm got lost, Frank thought—or maybe Joe had gotten caught up in the coral.

On the verge of panic Frank swam across the reef, desperate to find Joe and Malcolm. This is the crevice they went into—I think, Frank told himself as he swam into it.

An experienced diver, Frank knew that passages through reefs often took twists and turns. This one was no exception, and his lungs felt as though they were ready to burst.

Frank kicked forward, bending the upper part of his torso into the downward slant of the crevice. He saw a dark figure twitch in the shadows deep in the crevice.

Was it a body?

Was it Joe?

Frightened, Frank moved deeper into the crevice. Abruptly the figure hurtled through the water toward Frank.

Then he saw the shape more clearly. It was a set of jaws ringed with jagged, razor-sharp teeth—and it was moving forward to engulf Frank!

Chapter

10

THE JAWS SNAPPED shut inches in front of Frank's nose. He stared into the gruesomely ugly face of a moray eel!

Frank's heart raced. He had little oxygen left to retreat from the six-foot creature. Frank grasped an outcropping of coral, which snapped off in his hand. Without thinking he thrust the coral into the mouth of the onrushing eel. The eel chomped on it and began to thrash about wildly.

Frank felt something grip his ankle and tug. Panic-stricken, he turned, ready to give a mighty kick.

When he saw it was Joe, Frank let his body go limp, and Joe swiftly towed him to the surface.

"Are—you—okay?" Joe gasped as their heads broke the surface.

"No sweat," Frank panted.

"Are you boys all right?" Reeves called from his boat twenty yards away.

"We're okay," Joe said, and towed Frank back to his windsurfer. "Frank just got personal with a huge moray eel."

"They attack if you enter their territory," Reeves said somberly. "But it should leave you alone now."

"Malcolm, are you looking after these young men?" Reeves asked.

"I sure am, boss," Malcolm replied.

"Good," Reeves said. "See to it they don't miss their flight tomorrow morning."

"What makes you think we're planning to leave on that flight?" Frank protested, his voice still husky from his near-disaster.

Reeves studied him gravely. "If not, you would be well-advised to change your plans and take the flight," he said. He fired up his engine and pulled away from the boys.

"Where were you two?" Frank asked, lying on his windsurfer beside his brother and Malcolm. "I came to the surface just after Reeves passed by, then I went back down. I couldn't find you."

"We must have come to the surface just as you were going back under," Joe said. "When Reeves saw us thrashing around looking for you, he came out to see what was going on."

"And to give us another subtle hint about leaving," Frank said ruefully.

"You guys have got something against our president, don't you?" Malcolm asked.

"Let's just say I'd give anything to learn more about his private business," Frank said.

"Then wait a minute," Malcolm said with a sly smile. "I'll be right back."

He paddled into shore, to a spot near Reeves's pier. Frank saw him retrieve an object from behind the grass, stuff it into the waistband of his swimsuit, and paddle back toward them again.

"What's that?" Frank said as Malcolm handed him an accordion folder.

"When you were snooping around the front of Reeves's house, I went in the back door and grabbed this." He shrugged and grinned at Frank. "I thought maybe you'd want to give me something for it."

"All right!" Frank said, unable to contain his excitement. Frank reached for the folder, which Malcolm held just out of his grasp.

"How much?" he repeated with a smile.

After the Hardys agreed to give Malcolm a twenty-dollar bonus, the three of them began paddling back to the hotel.

"Give the folder back to me when you're finished with it," Malcolm advised Frank after they had ridden their boards onto the beach. "I'll slip it back into Reeves's."

"I hope what we're looking for is in here," Frank said, taking the folder from Malcolm.

"Me, too, boss," Malcolm said. Then he shrugged. "Maybe you'll give me another bonus."

"Just remember," Frank said, "there will be

a bonus only if you don't tell anyone a thing you know about us.''

"Who would I tell?" Malcolm asked.

"Your parents," Joe said.

"Don't have any parents," Malcolm said matter-of-factly as they rounded the side of the hotel.

"Then the people you live with," Frank said.

"I live alone," Malcolm declared.

"Where?" Joe asked.

"Wherever I choose," the boy said. Before Joe could respond he added, "See you tomorrow—at four A.M. sharp." Running away, he jumped on his scooter and took off, waving at passersby on all sides.

Joe shook his head. "The more we're around that kid, the less we know about him."

"And you know what's funny?" Frank added. "I don't care if he did try to steal our money. I like him. Come on. Let's grab a bite at that fruit stand, then look over these papers Malcolm swiped for us."

"This is boring," Joe groaned. It was hours later, and he and Frank had gone through most of Reeves's papers in their hotel room.

"Property tax assessments, records of import duties," Joe intoned, tossing aside stacks of papers. He took one sheaf from the stack. "Oh, here's a fascinating one," he joked. "A list of people who applied for fishing licenses this year!" He threw the papers down, stood up, and stretched.

"Hold on," Frank said. He was flipping through

the contents of a manila envelope he had found near the bottom of the stack.

"I've already been through that," Joe said. "It's just copies of a bunch of old newspaper clippings."

"But don't you see? They're about the Caribbean black market during World War II. And not just the Caribbean—Africa and South America, too," Frank replied, excitement in his voice.

"So?" Joe asked. "That was a long time ago."

"Exactly," Frank said. "He's looking for tips."

"Let's see those clips." Joe took some from Frank. "I don't know," he said. "These stories are about all kinds of illegal smuggling."

"Yeah, but wait a minute." Frank stared at one article. "I think I get it. All of these black market operations were run by one man. This one." Frank gave the article to Joe. It described the trial and conviction of Captain Roger Morgan, a young officer in the British Navy, on charges of masterminding a huge black market operation.

"He was one bad dude," Joe said, scanning the article.

"And look at this," Frank said. He held out another article to Joe.

"Morgan Escapes Prison," the headline read. "Notorious Black Marketeer on the Loose."

Joe let out a low whistle. "Do you think this guy could be Jolly Roger?"

"Why not?" Frank said, taking the clipping

back. "He'd be about seventy now, and that description could fit Reeves, Clarkston, or even Scobie. I can't believe there are no pictures of him here."

"Or he could be someone we haven't met yet," Joe added dejectedly. He shook his head. "Well, there's nothing we can do now to narrow the list of suspects. Let's get some sleep."

"I feel too wound up to drop right off to sleep. Do you think there's any chance of getting a glass of milk in this place?"

"I doubt that there's room service," Joe told him. "Maybe you could sneak down to the kitchen and get a glass."

Frank nodded. "I'll get you one, too," he said. "If there's one thing I can't stand, it's you tossing and turning all night when I'm trying to get my beauty sleep."

Moments later Frank was quietly heading downstairs and into the cool, dark hotel lobby. This deserted hotel was spooky, he thought.

Through the stillness, Frank heard the clatter of a keyboard. He peered into the office through a window and saw Miranda Watt bent over her computer.

Remembering how friendly she had been when the brothers had checked in that morning, Frank was tempted to keep her company. Then he remembered his early-morning plans and walked on to the kitchen. He poured two glasses of milk from a carton in the large refrigerator, then stole quietly out again. In the lobby, he paused a second time.

Miranda's office light was off. She must have finally gone to bed. Good idea, Frank thought.

"Who's there?" hissed a voice.

Frank froze, his heart pounding.

"Oh, it's you," said a feminine voice from the shadows. "You scared me."

"Miranda?" Frank asked.

"Yes, sorry," she said, moving toward Frank. "It's late. Why aren't you in bed?"

"We were thirsty." Sheepishly, Frank held up the glasses of milk. "You can put these on our bill."

"Don't be silly." Miranda laughed with relief. "You have no idea how you scared me. That would be all this place would need right now— a thief!"

"Where were you?" Frank asked. "I mean— I thought you had gone to bed."

"Just walking on the beach," Miranda told him. Frank couldn't help but admire how beautiful she was in the darkness. "It helps me when I'm feeling low."

"Business is that bad?"

"Oh, let's not talk about that," Miranda said, laughing shortly. "Let's talk about you." She paused. "Let's talk about what you're doing here. I—I know something terrible is going on on this island."

Frank stiffened, instantly suspicious.

"Strange men come through here every month

or so—stay a night, then leave on the first plane out," Miranda told him.

Of course, Frank thought. Couriers stayed at her hotel.

"They're unpleasant people," Miranda continued, "who look like criminals." She met Frank's eye. "Are you one of them? Will you tell me what's going on? This is my home."

Frank clutched the glasses of milk. She trusts me—but can I trust her? he asked himself. "No," he said. "Joe and I are staying on—we're just tourists. But I have a question for you. Do you know anything about a man named Captain Morgan?"

At the mention of Morgan's name, Miranda gasped.

"You're looking for Captain Morgan?" she asked.

"Yes," Frank said. "Do you know him?"

She stared at Frank, terror in her pale blue eyes.

"Yes," she whispered. "In fact, I saw him last night."

Chapter

11

"YOU SAW Captain Morgan?" Frank gasped. "Where? When?"

"Just after midnight, out there," Miranda said. "He was walking across the water, out to sea."

"He was walking on water?" Frank asked.

"His spirit was," Miranda explained. "Captain Henry Morgan died more than three hundred years ago."

Frank threw his head back and laughed. He realized she was talking about Henry Morgan, a bloodthirsty English pirate who had terrified the Caribbean back in the 1600s.

"What's so funny?" Miranda asked, sounding hurt.

"I'm sorry," Frank said. "It's just a case of mistaken identity."

"Ask anyone here," she said in utter seriousness. "His ghost haunts this island—and all the islands where he left his treasure."

"Old Captain Morgan left a treasure here?" Frank asked.

"They say he buried a treasure chest on Small Key back in 1674 and still searches for it on the anniversary of his death," Miranda said seriously.

Frank studied Miranda. It seemed odd that a woman like her would believe in ghosts. "You seem to know a lot about him."

"Of course I do," she said with a sly smile. "The spirits of the old Spanish Main are all around us." She gazed out a window at the moonlight beach. "That's the real reason I'll never leave this place."

Frank thought about Miranda Watt as he and Malcolm rode scooters down the road at dawn the next morning. Her fascination with pirates and ghosts struck Frank as weird. Was her fascination real?

Frank had left Joe in their room ten minutes earlier, telling Malcolm that Joe was too tired to get up. Frank knew that Joe would get into Clarkston's shanty and check it out once they were out to sea.

When they arrived at Clarkston's pier, they found the man on deck, lining up fishing poles against the cabin.

"Ahoy," Frank called as he and Malcolm walked down the pier. Except for Clarkston, there was no other sign of life.

"Good morning," Clarkston replied. "Where's your friend?"

"Dreamland." Frank followed Malcolm onto the boat. "I guess it'll be just the three of us."

Half an hour later the three of them were far out to sea. Frank sat in the stern of the boat, smiling at the antics of a large flock of sea gulls diving in the boat's wake. Clarkston cut the engines and joined Frank at the stern, helping him cast his lines.

Hoping to learn more about Clarkston's background, Frank asked, "Been long on Grand Key?"

"Long enough." Clarkston poured coffee from a large thermos into a cup.

"It seems like a beautiful spot," Frank said. "So unspoiled."

"Sure," Clarkston grumbled. "If you consider 'backward' the same as 'unspoiled.' "

Frank looked at Clarkston. "What do you mean?"

"I mean it's impossible to make a living here," Clarkston said bluntly. "It's depressing."

"Miranda Watt was saying the same thing yesterday," Frank said. "Why don't more people come here?"

"How can they?" Clarkston asked. "The water taxi from the Bahamas costs a fortune. They could fly their own planes—but how many people own planes? So they're stuck with one commercial flight a week."

"Isn't it President Reeves's fault that there's just one flight?" Frank asked.

Clarkston chuckled bitterly. "Not entirely. Ask your guide."

Frank turned toward Malcolm, who sat watching Frank with cold, emotionless eyes.

Joe peered back over his shoulder as he approached Clarkston's shanty. The only creature he saw was an old yellow dog scratching behind one ear.

Making sure no one was watching, Joe stealthily approached the door. Padlocked! He whipped his Swiss army knife out from his pocket and used the long, thin tweezers to work on the rusty lock.

Two minutes later Joe was inside. He glanced around the living room's spartan furnishings. Nothing seemed to have been moved from the day before—except that now the top of the desk was down, hiding Clarkston's high-tech equipment from view.

Joe went first to a low chest of drawers in the far corner of the room. Rummaging through the drawers, he found nothing but clothes. He was mildly surprised to discover that the bottom three drawers all contained colorful T-shirts advertising Grand Key and other Caribbean islands.

"That's funny," Joe muttered. Clarkston looked like the last guy to collect souvenir T-shirts.

"Okay," he said aloud. "On to the good stuff." He strode to the desk and lifted its roll-top. Beneath it were the combination phone and fax machine with a phone line feeding to a jack on the base of the wall. A laptop computer was tucked between the fax machine and a small dot matrix printer.

"If this isn't evidence, I don't know what is," Joe muttered, his heart pounding as he checked out the rest of the desktop. "He has all he needs to receive and place orders for the cars."

Joe glanced through the papers neatly filed in the pigeonholes above the desktop. All had to do with the operation of the fishing service.

He opened a drawer on the desk. "Bingo!" Joe cried, his pulse racing. The drawer was filled with new car magazines. Joe leafed through a few. Clarkston had circled the photos of a number of new sports and luxury cars.

Excited, Joe returned the magazines to the drawer. As he removed his hand, it brushed against something hard. Joe reached back in and pulled out a box of software. He opened it and took out several three-and-half-inch diskettes.

Joe smiled as he read the handwritten labels on each diskette.

Orders, one read.

Deliveries, read the other.

"We've got you now!" Joe said with a triumphant smile. "Jolly Roger or Morgan or whoever you are."

Quickly Joe turned on the computer and began to copy the data onto blank diskettes.

Just then he heard a faint noise from outside. "What was that?" he said, spinning around and running to a nearby window. He saw nothing.

"Must be my imagination—or a ghost," Joe muttered. He returned to the computer to finish copying the information he was sure would crack the car pirating ring wide open.

Less than two hours later, Frank, Malcolm, and Clarkston pulled up to Clarkston's dock. The boys headed down the pier, exhausted. Frank had struck out trying to get information from Clarkston. Except for grousing about the lack of tourism, Clarkston refused to say much to Frank.

Of course, a smuggling mastermind would be sure to keep his mouth shut.

Frank tried not to peek into the windows of Clarkston's shanty as they passed. Joe had had plenty of time to come and go by now, Frank told himself.

As soon as they were out of earshot of Clarkston, Malcolm turned to Frank. "Come on!" he said. "The weather is perfect for wind-surfing. We can sail out to—"

"Not so fast," Frank said, grabbing Malcolm by the shoulder. "I've got a few questions to ask you."

"Huh?" Malcolm asked, surprised.

"You heard what Clarkston told me about you on the boat," Frank told him. "He said if I wanted to know who was keeping tourists off Grand Key, I should ask you. What did he mean by that?"

"He's been spending too much time in the sun," Malcolm said.

"Don't play innocent with me, Malcolm," Frank said. "You're no dummy. You know something is terribly wrong on this island. Don't you? You know what's happening on Small Key." He stared deep into the boy's eyes.

"I know," Malcolm admitted with lowered eyes. "There are pirates."

"That's right." Frank let go of him, relieved. "Yesterday, you asked Joe and me what we were doing here. Well, we're here to put the pirates behind bars."

"So—what does that have to do with me and tourists?" Malcolm objected.

"The pirates don't want the tourists here," Frank told him. "Someone might find out what they're up to. If you have something to do with keeping people away—then we have to wonder if you're involved."

Malcolm stared at Frank angrily. "You think I'm a pirate?"

"Malcolm, I don't know what you are."

Malcolm sighed deeply. "Follow me. I want to show you something," he said, walking over to their scooters. Frank followed.

Malcolm led Frank to a low building across from the immigration booth. The building bore a sign reading Post Office and Town Hall.

"Good morning, Malcolm," called an elderly man, sorting letters behind a counter.

"Hello, Mr. Keaton," Malcolm called back to the man. He crossed the room to a large bulletin board on the far wall. Dozens of sheets of paper were tacked onto the wall and protected by a sheet of Plexiglas. Know Your Laws! read a hand-lettered sign tacked above it.

"What does this have to do with anything?" Frank asked impatiently.

"This is Grand Key's entire law book, man," Malcom explained. "Here, that's the one you want, I think." He pointed to a sheet in the middle.

"Code Four-four-five, Section Five—The Malcolm Bradbury Act," Frank read. "No more than a single commercial flight shall be allowed to land at the Grand Key Airport in any given calendar week."

Frank looked with surprise at his young companion. "The act is named after you?" he asked.

"Sure is," Malcolm said mildly.

"Why is that?" Frank asked.

"I'm the one who asked for it," Malcolm said, his voice cracking slightly. "I carried a petition around the island, and everyone who was born here signed it."

"Why?" Frank asked, perplexed.

"We don't want a lot of tourists here!" Malcolm said sharply. He turned away, but not before Frank saw tears welling up in the boy's eyes.

"My father used to take tourists out in his boat," Malcolm said bitterly. "We were always friendly to them. Then my father took a group out on the boat with him. There was an accident—"

Frank moved toward Malcolm to console him, but the boy stepped away.

"My father never came home that day," Malcolm concluded, a sob in his voice.

"Malcolm!" Frank ran after the boy as he rushed out the door, but he had already jumped on his scooter. As Malcolm started the bike, Frank grabbed him by the shoulders.

"Malcolm—I'm sorry about your father," Frank said. "Please—don't be mad."

Malcolm started the motor and peered into Frank's face. "I'm not mad," he said through his tears. "I'm scared."

"Scared?" Frank stared at him. "Of what?"

"It wasn't my idea to ask for that law," Malcolm said. "I was paid to do it."

"Who paid you?" Frank asked, shocked.

Malcolm didn't answer. He sped down the road and out of town, as if pursued by a demon.

Joe lay on his bed, half asleep, thinking about how surprised Frank would be when Joe produced Mac Clarkston's computer disks. Frank would immediately ask to borrow Miranda Watt's computer, Joe mused, and less than ten minutes after that they would have proof of Mac Clarkston's guilt. Then they could hand Jolly Roger over to Special Agent Skinner, accept her heartfelt thanks and congratulations, and spend the rest of the week working on their tans.

The more he thought about it, the more impatient he grew for Frank to arrive. On the other hand, getting up at four in the morning had made him very tired. Just as Joe began to drift off to sleep, a noise jerked him awake.

It was his stomach grumbling. "Okay, okay. I'll get some breakfast," he groaned.

He decided to go to the fruit stand, and patted his pockets for money. "No," he said aloud. "Frank has all the money!"

Wait a second! Joe thought, glancing up at the ceiling lamp. He'd almost forgotten—the Hardys had a fortune at their disposal.

Joe dragged the desk chair over to a spot directly under the lamp. He stood on the chair and reached up into the open glass globe, his fingers feeling over the edge for the envelope.

He groped some more. There was nothing there. Panicked, Joe realized the money was gone!

At that instant Joe heard the roar of a motor scooter's engine and someone yelling outside. It was Frank's voice. After leaping off the chair, he ran to the balcony. Below, Joe saw Malcolm speeding down the sandy road behind the hotel with Frank on foot in hot pursuit.

As Joe watched, Frank stopped running in front of a shed and bent over, hands on knees, gasping for breath.

"Frank!" Joe yelled down from the window. Frank looked up as Joe caught sight of something flash below and to his left. He stared hard to see what it was.

From his position on the balcony, Joe could look along the entire facade of the hotel. A long, thin, metal shaft was sticking out from behind the corner of the building to his left. It was a trident of some kind, with barbed hooks on its tip.

A spear gun! Joe realized with a gasp.

"Frank! Duck!" Joe yelled. Just then the spear was set loose and whizzed through the air directly at his brother's heart.

Chapter

12

THWOCK!

Frank screamed with pain.

At his brother's warning to duck, Frank had instinctively doubled over. In the next instant he felt an icy slash along the small of his back, then he heard the sound of metal hitting wood.

Frank tried to run to safety, but was pinned in place. He turned his head to see the spear quivering in the wooden wall of the shed.

"Whew!" Frank stared, amazed at how close he'd come to becoming a human shish kebab. As it was, his back burned where the tip had grazed him and his shirt was pinned to the door.

Frank tried to pull himself free, but his shirt had him trapped. "Joe!" Frank called. "Joe!"

"I'm here," Joe said, breathless, as he rushed to Frank's side. "Oh—you're bleeding."

"Never mind," Frank said as Joe jerked the spear from the door, freeing him. "Get the shooter."

"Right." Joe rushed off toward the left side of the building.

Still shaken, Frank walked gingerly toward the rear entrance of the hotel. As he reached the back porch, Frank spotted Miranda Watt in a flour-covered apron, watching him from the doorway.

"What happened?" she demanded, staring at Frank.

"Just a little accident," Frank said.

"Accident?" Miranda rushed to help Frank. Frank grimaced as she placed her hand on his back, helping him in.

"You've been badly cut!" she said.

"It's nothing," he insisted.

"Don't be ridiculous. You need attention. Come on, I'll clean and bandage you up." As she led him inside, Frank heard footsteps.

"Whoever it was got away," Joe said, joining them. "But he dropped this." He held out the speargun.

"Handle it carefully," Frank said. "We may be able to get prints off it."

"Wait a minute," Miranda said. She peered at the stock of the spear gun in Joe's hands. "Look—what does that lettering say?"

Joe turned the gun around to look at the stock. Carved into it were two letters. "MC," Joe read. He looked at Frank significantly.

"Mac Clarkston!" they said in unison.

"Ouch!" Frank yelped out, lying facedown across his bed.

"I know it stings," Miranda said, dabbing his back with iodine. "But it's necessary. Who knows what bacteria were on that spear?"

Joe watched anxiously as Miranda cleaned and dressed Frank's wound. He wanted her to be finished—and fast. He had to tell Frank about the missing money.

As Miranda stuck down the last bit of tape a loud roar filled the room. Joe put his hands over his ears and looked overhead.

"What's that?" he asked.

"That was the weekly flight leaving the airport," she said. "You should have been on that flight. Seems someone has it in for you."

"Don't worry about us," Joe said. "We can take care of ourselves."

"Fine," Miranda said, exasperated. "You macho boys take care of yourselves, but I'm reporting this attack to Scobie right away. I won't have people spearing each other outside my hotel!"

Miranda stormed out of the room. Joe rushed to the door and listened to her departing footsteps.

"Frank," he blurted out as soon as she was gone, "the money is missing!"

"What?" Frank looked up at the ceiling lamp. "Who—how?"

"Clarkston," Joe said. "Who else? He's got to be behind all this. Think about it." Joe ticked off points on his fingers. "When we showed up at his place asking to go fishing, he realized we were his couriers. When you showed up to go fishing this morning, he knew we planned to stick around. As far as he's concerned, no courier would stay longer than was necessary on Grand Key unless he planned to get J.R. He must have sent someone to snitch the money this morning and decided to take care of us the first time he caught us alone."

Frank considered this. "You're making too many guesses," he said. "We still don't have any proof."

"No proof?" Joe asked in disbelief. "What about that spear gun?"

"Anyone could have stolen that," Frank said. "We don't know for sure that the initials MC stand for Mac Clarkston. We need more evidence."

This was the moment Joe had been waiting for. He savored it as he pulled Mac Clarkston's two diskettes from his pocket. "How about this?" he asked, waving the disks in front of Frank. "These are copies of the ones I found at Clarkston's, along with a major stack of sports car magazines. These disks were labeled, Frank. One was marked Orders, the other Deliveries."

Frank stared at the disks. "You're sure these are records of stolen cars?"

"Sure I'm sure."

They were interrupted by a loud pounding at the door.

"Open up!" demanded a voice.

Joe crossed to the door and threw it open. The man who had stamped their passports the previous day entered, brandishing a revolver. Chief Scobie and Jordan Reeves followed—both very serious and very angry.

"The game is up, you two," boomed Reeves in his deep voice.

"What game?" Joe was trying to make sense of this new intrusion.

"I think you know," Reeves told him curtly. Turning to Scobie, he ordered, "Do it."

Scobie, all trace of friendliness erased, stepped forward, his gun drawn.

"Frank Goldstein and Joseph Burnside," Scobie recited sternly. "I hereby arrest you in the name of the sovereign government of Grand Key."

Joe's jaw dropped open. "On what charge?"

"Smuggling," Scobie said grimly. Frank and Joe were bewildered.

"You're nuts," Joe cried.

"Yeah," Frank seconded with an uneasy chuckle. "What evidence do you have?"

"All the evidence we need." Scobie held out the envelope containing the fifty thousand dollars. "We found it up there." He pointed to the ceiling lamp. "We saw its silhouette against the glass globe," he told them. "Next time, you should work harder at covering your tracks."

"Who's your boss?" Scobie asked Joe for about the hundredth time. "Who put you up to this?"

"I'm telling you, we're not smugglers," Joe said. "We're here on vacation."

After their arrest, Frank and Joe had been taken to the only prison cell on the island, located far out of the village on the road to the airport. It was an old, one-room stone building with a heavy wooden door and iron bars over the two small windows. A single metal bench was chained to the wall—otherwise the cell was empty. Frank, looking at the damp, heavy stone walls and thick door, guessed that the cell must date back hundreds of years.

To Henry Morgan's day, Frank thought wryly.

As soon as they had arrived at the cell, Scobie began interrogating the Hardys. Reeves watched from the corner and the immigration officer stood guard. It had been going on for hours.

"You criminals have made our island your way station for too long," Scobie said, his face flushed with anger. "I'm telling you now—we do not intend to put up with it anymore."

"We're not criminals!" Joe repeated hotly. "We've never been here before in our lives!"

While Joe argued with his interrogator, Frank's mind raced. It was clear from their questions that Scobie and Reeves already knew a lot about the smuggling operation. If they knew so much, why hadn't they shut it down, he wondered? Perhaps their official roles were only a front in this case, Frank realized. It was possible that these two men ran the operation themselves. They could have arrested the Hardys to make them disappear legally. Frank sensed that J.R.—whoever that was—would do anything to keep the pirating operation under his control.

Maybe they were in earnest, though, Frank thought. Maybe they truly were afraid of the smugglers and desperately wanted to be rid of them.

Frank ran over in his mind the clues they had unearthed so far. He considered the spear gun, the diskettes, the newspaper clippings, and Malcolm's confession earlier that day. Taking a deep breath, he chose a clue and decided to gamble.

"If you're so worried about your precious island," he blurted out, "why don't you go after the leader of the operation—Captain Roger Morgan?"

President Reeves rocked back on his heels, clearly stunned by Frank's mention of the old smuggler's name. At the same time Chief Scobie's eyes lit up. He moved closer to Frank.

"What do you know about Morgan?" he demanded, peering into Frank's eyes.

"Enough," Frank bluffed. "I first heard his name back when—"

"No!" Reeves roared before Frank could finish. "Enough talk!"

"But, Reeves, old man," Scobie protested, "if we ever hope to destroy these villains we must know—"

"If we hope to destroy them, Reggie, there is only one way," Reeves said. "No more cowering. We have to face our fears head-on."

"But—when?" Scobie asked him.

"Tonight! Let these boys rot in this cell. We'll raid Small Key and destroy those pirates once and for all."

Abruptly, Reeves turned and left the cell. "But—but—" Scobie said to the departing president. He followed Reeves from the cell. The immigration officer also left, sneering at the Hardys before slamming the door shut behind him. Frank and Joe rushed to the cell window and watched their three interrogators leave in the jeep that had brought them to the prison.

"What was that all about?" Joe asked, perplexed.

"I think I know," Frank said. "Don't you see? This person Morgan is running the car piracy ring. Reeves says he wants to smash the pirates—but he wants to protect Morgan."

"I get it," Joe said. "Scobie is trying to break up the smuggling ring, but Reeves won't let him. Do you think Reeves is Morgan?"

"If he is, he's not leading Scobie out to Small Key to arrest the smugglers. He's taking Scobie out to be killed."

"And that means we're sitting ducks in this cell, too," Joe declared.

He strode to the door and kicked it violently. It didn't even budge.

"If only there was some way out of here," Joe said, fighting panic. "I'd give anything to get that door open right now."

"I wouldn't," Frank said. "If that door were to open, it would probably be because Reeves ordered one of his killers to come and—"

Frank stopped short. He had heard a noise outside the prison door. Instantly alert, he and Joe turned to face the intruder.

Frank swallowed hard. The rusted hinges creaked as the ancient door squeaked open.

Chapter

13

"HEY, BOSS. What's up?"

It was Malcolm. Frank heaved a sigh of relief as the young boy entered the room from outside. "Malcolm!" he said. "How did you get the door open?"

Malcolm held up an open penknife. "Piece of cake," he said.

"Boy, are we glad it's you," Frank said.

"You won't be in a minute," Malcolm said angrily.

"We won't?" Frank looked at him uneasily. "What do you mean?"

"I mean you haven't paid me yet," Malcolm declared, "and I've come to collect my money."

"Is that all?" Joe patted Malcolm on the back as he strode out the door to get some air. "Don't worry," he said. "We'll pay you before we go. You can trust us."

"I know," Malcolm said. "That's why I brought you this." He took a carefully folded piece of paper from his pants pocket and gave it to Frank.

"What is it?" Frank asked, unfolding it. It was dog-eared and stained, covered with neat typewriting.

"That's my law," Malcolm explained. "It was given to me by the guy who asked me to start the petition. He told me to copy it in my own handwriting before I took it around to be signed."

"Who gave you this?" Frank asked, his pulse racing with excitement.

"He said to call him Razz," Malcolm explained. "He paid me what he promised, but I still know he's bad. He has a smile like death. Gold, right here." Malcolm tapped one of his teeth.

Frank nodded eagerly. "We've met him," he told Malcolm. "Joe, come back in here!" he called.

Joe returned. Frank filled him in on Malcolm's story—how the boy had been used by the pirates to get a law limiting tourist flights to the island, and how Razz had set it up.

"Do you think Razz could be running the whole show?" Joe asked Malcolm.

"Razz?" Malcolm laughed. "He's bad, but he's dumb, too. No, he works for someone else."

"Who?" Frank asked.

Malcolm shrugged his shoulders.

"There's one way to find out," Joe observed. "Stick around here till they show up armed and ready to bump us off!"

"Good point." Frank turned to Malcolm and gave him back the paper. "Reeves, Scobie, and another officer are heading out to Small Key. They're going to try arresting Razz and the others."

Malcolm's eyes grew wide. "They'll get slaughtered. Those guys kill for fun."

"Malcolm, do you know any way to get to the lagoon on Small Key," Joe asked, "besides using the ocean side?"

"Sure," Malcolm said. "My father and I used to hunt conch there. I know paths that lead across the island—better than Razz, I bet."

"Good," Frank said, leading them out into the cool dusk air. "Now, if we just had a boat—"

Malcolm grinned as he leapt onto his scooter. "That could be arranged," he said.

Night was falling as Malcolm steered the motorboat across the water toward Small Key. Frank sat beside Malcolm in the boat's stern, while Joe sat in the bow, the stiff ocean breeze hard against his face.

"It's a good thing your uncle lets you use his boat whenever you want," Frank called over the roar of the motor.

"Well, he doesn't exactly let me use it," Malcolm admitted. "I more or less borrowed it, if you know what I mean."

Moments later Malcolm guided the motorboat between two coral reef islands. Frank realized where Malcolm was taking them. The logical route to take from Grand Key to Small Key would be to head west from the larger island and go around the southern side of Small Key to the lagoon. Malcolm, however, was cutting between the chain of islets linking the two main islands, and would be approaching Small Key from the northwest.

The first stars were appearing when Joe pointed straight ahead.

"Small Key," he called, turning back to Frank and Malcolm.

Frank saw the rocky crown of Small Key rising out of the water.

"I know a good landing place," Malcolm said, steering the boat toward the island.

"Good," Joe said. "Then we have to get to the lagoon."

"I can get us there," Malcolm said. "Then what?"

"Then," Joe said with a cocky shrug, "we'll improvise."

"We will do no such thing," Frank said pointedly. He turned to Malcolm. "Joe and I will go to the lagoon—*alone*. It's no place for a kid, Malcolm."

"But—" Malcolm protested. Frank stopped him by holding up his hand.

"I mean it," he said. "Anyway, we need you to stay with the motorboat in case we need to make a quick getaway."

"Well—all right," Malcolm said with great reluctance. "But I don't know how you two will manage without me."

Malcolm steered the boat toward a section of the island covered with heavy foliage and beached it on a ribbon of sandy beach. "There," he said, pointing to a thin break in the trees and creepers. "That path leads to the far side of the island and the lagoon. It comes out just behind the old building there."

"Great." Joe leapt onto the sand. "How long will it take us to get there?"

"About five minutes."

"Okay," Frank said, joining his brother on the beach. "Wait for us for twenty minutes. If we're not back by then, go back to Grand Key. And if you hear anything that sounds like we're in danger, head straight back as well. Do not— I repeat—do not go to the lagoon."

"Sure, boss," Malcolm said. "But what sort of things should I be listening for?"

Just then a gunshot from the far side of the island shattered the stillness of the evening.

"Listen for something like that," Joe said, entering the trail. "Come on, Frank. We're wasting time."

The path the Hardys followed was little more than a slit through the heavily overgrown foliage on the island. Branches and vines cut Joe's face as he broke into a run, then sprinted through the underbrush until he suddenly burst into a clearing. Before him stood the rear corner of the old metal warehouse, nearly invisible beneath a thick blanket of creepers. An instant later Frank joined him behind the building. They paused for a moment in the silence of the clearing. Then they heard a voice from beyond the warehouse, amplified as though the speaker were using an electric bullhorn.

"We repeat—this is your last chance. Give yourselves up!"

"It's Reeves," Joe whispered to Frank, surprised. "Why would he threaten the smugglers if he was on their side?"

Before Frank could respond, the gunfire resumed—louder and more prolonged than before. Frank and Joe threw themselves up against the side of the building. Crouching down, they slunk toward the front of the building, passing the old wooden door in the building's rear wall.

As he reached the front corner, Joe peered cautiously around. The fools! he thought, seeing the situation Scobie and Reeves had gotten themselves into.

Razz and four other men were crouched behind the pylons on the dock, directly in front of the warehouse. The warehouse doors were half open to allow the gunmen to enter and replenish their ammunition. It was a good siege position, Joe realized. The smugglers could hold out as long as their ammunition lasted.

Scobie and Reeves, however, were in deep trouble. They were crouched in a speedboat in the middle of the harbor—sitting ducks. It was only a matter of time before the smugglers' fire shot their boat full of holes.

Time! In a flash Joe knew what they should do.

"Let's buy Scobie some time," he murmured to Frank. "We can get into the warehouse and steal the smugglers' ammunition."

"I'm right behind you," Frank said.

The Hardys carefully retraced their steps to the wooden door in the back of the warehouse. Joe swung it open and entered the shadowy garage. A lit hurricane lamp dangled from a beam near the center of the warehouse, revealing the gleaming cars parked tidily along the back wall of the warehouse. Joe peered around until he spotted, against the opposite wall, an open wooden crate. The ammo! Joe realized.

As Frank waited, Joe peered through the half open door at the loading dock. The shooting had momentarily stopped. Joe scurried across the concrete floor, followed by Frank.

"Can we carry it?" Frank asked as they wrapped their arms around the crate.

"We can try," Joe said. Straining, they managed to lift the crate off the floor and began to haul it toward the back door. They were halfway there when a new burst of gunfire exploded outside. A stray bullet chipped the floor ten feet in front of them.

"Duck!" Frank whispered. The Hardys dropped the crate on the floor and scrambled to hide among the parked cars.

"What now?" Joe muttered, exasperated. Just then, he heard a voice from the dock.

"Clarence, I'm out of rounds. Get more ammunition!"

Joe ducked down. He heard the clatter of footsteps as one of the five gunmen entered the warehouse. There was a brief moment of silence. Then—

"Hey! What's going on?" a voice called out.

Joe's gaze whipped around to meet Frank's. The gunman saw that the ammunition had been moved and was looking for them!

"Who's there?" the voice called out. His heart pounding, Joe remained silent and in a low crouch. Frank did the same.

Joe watched a pair of legs move in front of him as Clarence walked past the row of cars. Tensing his muscles, Joe leapt out from behind his car, taking down the intruder in a flying tackle.

"Watch out, Joe!" Frank yelled as Joe tumbled to the floor, struggling to keep the man's gun from firing in his face. As the two wrestled on the floor the gun went off, spraying bullets against the warehouse ceiling.

Suddenly Joe heard the sound of glass breaking. Then a loud whoosh seemed to pass through the room. "Joe! Run!" Frank yelled as Joe turned to see the hurricane lamp spilling blue flames as its fuel spread a lake of fire on the floor.

Before Joe could react, his own head exploded with a burst of light.

"Aagh," Joe cried as he collapsed to the floor. He shook his head groggily as Clarence sprinted out the back door, still clutching the gun with which he'd bludgeoned Joe.

His head spinning, Joe raised his head.

The pool of blue flame was spreading.

In an instant it would reach the box of ammunition on the floor, inches from Joe's face!

Chapter

14

"IT'S GOING to blow!" Joe yelled as a car engine roared to life behind him.

He saw Frank sitting behind the wheel of the Mercedes-Benz convertible they had stolen days before. "Get in!" Frank shouted.

Joe scrambled to his feet and rushed to the car, vaulting over the door as Frank dropped the car into gear. Joe was tossed against the car seat as the Benz shot forward, tires screaming on the concrete floor.

The car sped through the warehouse. As they shot past the box of ammunition, Joe saw that it was already engulfed in blue flames.

"Duck!" he yelled, crouching low in the seat. He peered up out the windshield as Frank directed the car out the main warehouse door.

As the car burst through the doors, a tremendous explosion filled Joe's ears. He saw the gunmen on the dock turn and jump out of the Hardys' way as the Benz careened down the dock and arced gracefully through the air. Joe vaulted out of his seat as the car dropped into the water. A moment later he splashed into the lagoon. An instant later the Benz slammed into the water, too.

Thrashing to the water's surface, Joe searched wildly for his brother. "Frank?" he called. The Mercedes was half submerged in the water beside him. No one was in the driver's seat.

"Frank?" Joe yelled again, panic in his voice.

"Here," came a reassuring reply. In the darkness, Joe spotted Frank treading water on the far side of the car. Greatly relieved, he grinned at his brother.

"Too bad it doesn't have air bags to make it float," Joe said. "Otherwise we could drive this baby home."

Frank laughed and looked back at the dock. The exploding ammunition had almost leveled the warehouse—most of the roof was scattered in the surrounding trees, and the walls were pockmarked with dents and holes. The dock was clear of gunmen.

"They all scattered," Frank called out. "Now it's just a question of mopping up—"

"Put your hands where we can see them," boomed an amplified voice. Frank turned to see the police boat approaching. Scobie stood at the bow, speaking through a bullhorn. His deputy stood beside him, pointing a gun in the Hardys' direction. "You two are under arrest," he said.

Then he got a closer look at his captives. "Not you guys again. We just saved you," he said, as the deputy fished them out of the water. "And what were you doing in the warehouse?" Scobie asked. "Destroying evidence?"

Frank scrambled on board the boat. "We were sneaking up on them in order to help you out."

"That's your story?" Reeves shook his head. He was standing near the back of the boat, watching the Hardys suspiciously. "I'm afraid you two will have to do better than that."

"I think we will," Frank said, peering off at the mouth of the lagoon. Joe heard the low, throaty rumble of a boat's engine. He followed the direction of Frank's gaze.

Through the darkness he could make out Malcolm steering his boat into the lagoon. He was followed closely by a large, streamlined motorboat. A muscular man stood at its helm, but Joe didn't give him a second glance. Standing beside the man was Special Agent Skinner of the FBI, and the rumpled shape beside her was Fenton Hardy.

"Let me get this straight," Reeves said wearily to Skinner. "These two boys really are FBI agents?"

"Not exactly, but close enough," the young agent replied with a smile at the brothers. "Your father insisted on coming along," she added to them. "I told him you could take care of yourselves."

It was an hour after the explosion, and Reeves, Skinner, and the three Hardys were on their way back to Grand Key on Skinner's boat, accompanied by three FBI field agents. Four of the smugglers huddled, handcuffed, in the rear of the boat.

"It's lucky you showed up when you did," Frank said, glancing at the smugglers. "You and your fellow agents had the manpower we needed to nab these thugs."

"You did a good day's work, boys," Fenton said to his sons. "I hate to tell you this, but the party's over. After Agent Skinner heard your report yesterday, Frank, she decided to round up Ambler and his crew. Now the police need you two to testify against them as eyewitnesses.

"Why crack down so soon?" Frank asked Agent Skinner. "When J.R. finds out that Ambler was busted, he'll know the jig is up."

"Exactly," Skinner said. "We timed his arrest—and the arrests of all his other hijacking rings we know about in the States—to occur at the time we arrived here. We're betting that the news will flush out the head pirate. At the dock, a fisherman named Clarkston told us the police boat left for Small Key."

"Clarkston *must* be running the show," Joe said. "That's why he sent you out to the island— to give him a chance to make his getaway!"

Skinner frowned. "He *was* preparing his boat to go out to sea," she said.

To Joe's surprise, Reeves suddenly smiled.

"You mean Clarkston is behind this smuggling ring?" he said, relief in his voice.

Officer Scobie shook his head. "Impossible," he said as the boat approached one of the docks at Grand Key Harbor. "I've known Mac Clarkston for too many years. He's a grouch, I'll admit, but as honest as the day is long."

Joe stared at Scobie in disbelief. Could it be that the police chief had no idea what his old friend had been up to all these years? Or was Scobie covering for Clarkston in the hope that the suspicion would pass?

One thing was for sure, Joe realized. No one could go after Clarkston until they had convincing evidence. As the boat sidled up to the dock, Joe vaulted over the railing and onto the wooden pier.

"Hey! Where do you think you're going?" Skinner called after him.

"Come on, Frank," Joe called with a wave at the others. Over his shoulder he saw Frank jump off the boat as well and race after Joe toward the Grand Hotel.

Out of breath by the time he reached the hotel, Joe bounded up the front steps two at a time—almost knocking over Miranda Watt. She was just exiting the front door, her head wrapped in a stylish silk bandanna.

"Whoa, there!" she gasped.

"Sorry," Joe said as he rushed past her.

Then Joe stopped and called back to her. "Excuse me, Miranda," he said. "Could I use your computer for a few minutes?"

Miranda's face broke into a grin.

"Of course," she said. "Make yourself at home."

Thanking her, Joe rushed upstairs to their room, found the diskettes he had taken from Clarkston's desk, and ran back downstairs. There he found Frank and the others milling about the lobby in confusion.

"What have you got there?" Skinner demanded. "What's going on?"

"Spreadsheets." Joe held up the diskettes. "They were on Clarkston's computers. One reads Orders, and the other Deliveries. I'm telling you, he's our man!"

"Let's take a look at those." Skinner took the diskettes from Joe. "I have a laptop with my luggage down at the airport."

"Miranda said we could use the hotel computer," Joe told her excitedly, leading them to the office behind the lobby.

Frank followed Joe. "Frank, you know your way around a spreadsheet," Joe said, switching on the computer. "You do the honors."

Frank sat at the keyboard as the rest of the group gathered around him. He slipped one diskette into the computer's floppy drive, then called up the hard drive directory.

"Does she have a spreadsheet program?" Skinner asked.

"She should, if she's running a hotel. There it is," Frank said, recognizing the software's directory. He called up the program.

"Okay, Clarkston, let's see your evil book-keeping," Joe muttered as Frank's fingers flew over the keyboard.

"This data I'm calling up is from Clarkston's Orders directory," Frank explained.

Words and numbers filled the empty slots on the screen. Everyone leaned forward to read it.

" 'Nassau—fifty-two extra larges,' " Scobie read.

" 'Antigua—one hundred four mediums,' " Skinner read.

" 'Barbados—two hundred twenty-five larges,' " Reeves read.

"Wait a minute," Joe said in shocked surprise. "These orders aren't for cars. They're for T-shirts!"

"That's right," roared a deep voice behind them. "And they're mine!"

Chapter

15

FRANK SWIVELED AROUND in the chair. Mac Clarkston's bulky body filled the office doorway.

"I was wondering who had been monkeying around with my computer," he said, turning to Joe. "You left the diskettes on my desk."

"Clarkston!" Reeves said. "We thought you'd run away."

"Run away?" Clarkston replied. "I took a spin to check on some crawfish traps I'd set. I saw Reeves and Scobie rush in here and thought I'd make sure everything was all right."

"Let me get this straight," Joe said, red-faced. "You run a T-shirt importing business?"

"Distribution business is more like it," Clarkston corrected Joe. "They're printed in Florida. I take orders from tourist shops around the Caribbean and have the shirts shipped.''

''But''— sputtered Joe. ''What about the automobile magazines I saw in your desk?''

''You're a real snoop, aren't you?'' Clarkston said.

''Mac used to work as an automotive designer,'' Scobie said. ''He came here to get away from the ratrace.''

As the others talked, Frank typed on the computer, idly exploring its directory. No matter what Miranda Watt said about Grand Key's low-tech condition, this was one great computer, he realized. With a 25 megahertz speed and 120 megabyte hard drive it was nearly as powerful as his own—and this one had a laser printer as well.

A laser printer, Frank thought. A laser printer that produces neat type—

He jumped from the chair and began going through a vertical file on a shelf above the computer.

''What are you looking for?'' Fenton asked him.

''This.'' Frank took a piece of paper from the folder.

Joe studied the paper. ''It's just the copy of a letter she wrote to order some towels.''

''Wait a minute.'' Frank scanned the room until he saw Malcolm in the rear. ''Malcolm,'' he called. ''Can I take another look at that paper you showed me earlier?''

''Sure,'' Malcolm replied, making his way to

Frank. He took the worn sheet from his pocket and handed it over. "Here's my law," he said.

Frank turned to Joe. "Now compare the type for Malcolm's law to the towel order," he told his brother.

"The type matches perfectly!" Joe exclaimed.

Frank sat in front of the computer and began to type, closing down the spreadsheet and getting back to the computer's hard drive directory.

"I'm lost." Skinner turned from the papers to Malcolm. "What do these have to do with anything?"

"They think that whoever wrote this paper is the leader," Malcolm told her.

"Right," said Frank. "And the type matches the type produced by this laser printer!"

"It could be a coincidence," Reeves said, his voice thick with anxiety.

"Are you kidding?" Joe retorted. "Take a look around—how many printers are on this island?"

"What are you looking for now, son?" Fenton was peering over Frank's shoulder at the screen.

"This," Frank said with satisfaction. He pointed at a directory labeled Private.

"You have no right to look in there," Reeves said as Frank tried to open the directory. "That's Miranda's personal property."

"He may not have the right," Skinner snapped at Reeves. "But he has the backing. Go ahead, kid. Open the file."

"I can't," Frank moaned, still typing. "I have to know the password to get it open."

"A password?" Joe asked. "What could a hotelkeeper have on her computer that's so private?"

"What about Grand Key?" Malcolm spoke up excitedly. "Or Grand Hotel?"

Frank tried both, but neither worked.

All at once Frank broke into a smile. "I've got it," he said. He typed in the letters *M, O, R, G, A, N.*
The directory opened immediately. "Yes!" Frank said in triumph as the others—except for Jordan Reeves—crowded closer. Frank reopened the spreadsheet and called up one of the documents from the private directory.

Joe whistled. "Look at that," he said. On the screen were listed dozens of luxury cars. In the columns next to them were listed destinations in Africa, South America, and the Caribbean.

"We got her," Joe said, pounding the desk with his fist. Joe turned, startled, as someone let out a loud groan. Jordan Reeves slumped in a chair, his head buried in his hands. Scobie stood beside him, his hand on Reeves's shoulder.

"I tried to tell you, old man," he muttered softly. "I tried to tell you."

"Miranda Watt is a smuggler," Mac Clarkston said, shaking his head in disbelief. "I never would have believed it. I just passed her on my way here from the harbor," Clarkston remembered. "She said she'd be back in half an hour."

"The harbor?" Frank scrambled to his feet. "Maybe there's still time to stop her!"

With the others trailing behind, Frank sprinted from the hotel to the darkened piers of the harbor. He saw the lights of a large speedboat reflecting off the water as it darted for the open sea. As he approached the dock, Frank saw the immigration officer sitting propped against a pylon, rubbing his head.

"What happened?" Frank asked the man as Joe rushed up alongside him.

"Miranda hit me with a gun," the officer explained. "She was meeting a man in that speed boat."

"Who?" Scobie joined them, out of breath after his run to the dock.

"I didn't recognize him," the deputy said. "He had a gold tooth," he added, tapping one of his own.

"Razz," Joe said as Agent Skinner, Mac Clarkston, and Fenton arrived.

"You can forget about catching her," Clarkston said, shaking his head as he watched the departing speedboat. "Miranda's boat is the fastest one on the islands."

Nevertheless, Joe and Scobie trotted to the end of the dock. Scobie jumped into the police boat and he took his bullhorn from the seat.

"Stop," Scobie bellowed into the bullhorn. "You can't escape, Miranda. Stop before it's too late."

"Fire a warning shot," Joe suggested. Scobie slipped his gun from its holster and aimed into the air directly over the fleeing boat.

"Stop," he repeated into the bullhorn. "Stop or I'll shoot!" Then he pulled the trigger on the gun.

Ka-boom!

A split second after Scobie's shot, Miranda Watt's boat exploded in a tremendous fireball. The powerful blast sent Joe sprawling on the dock. Looking up, he saw flaming pieces of the boat drop into the harbor around the burning, splintered hull.

Scobie was staring at the wreck, too, his face ashen. "I guess I aimed too low," he murmured.

"It's hard to believe that Miranda was the brains behind the car pirating ring," Scobie said. An hour later the Hardys were sitting in Watt's office with their father, Agent Skinner, and Scobie. Malcolm, exhausted, had crept upstairs for a nap. Reeves was alone in the dark lobby.

"We knew something had been going on on Small Key," Scobie continued, "but I couldn't convince Reeves that Miranda was involved."

"How long did you suspect her?" Frank asked.

"I had my doubts about her as soon as she and her husband bought this hotel two years ago."

"Two years ago?" Joe said. "She told us her husband built it twenty years ago."

"Then she lied," Scobie said. "They bought it together, summer before last. Shortly after that, the mysterious ships began arriving at Small Key, and shady characters began passing through our island."

"Couriers," Frank said. "And it was about that time Malcolm got his law passed, right?"

"Correct," Scobie said.

"What happened to Watt's husband?" Skinner asked.

"Died of a heart attack about eighteen months ago," Scobie said. "He was at least thirty years older than her. Like I say, I suspected that they were involved in whatever was going on out at Small Key, so I began to look into Mr. Watt's past."

"And that led you to Captain Morgan?" Frank asked.

"Yes," Scobie said with a nod. "A buddy of mine at Scotland Yard sent me information on a notorious smuggler named Roger Morgan who's been at large since the end of the war. No one knew what happened to him, but it was believed he continued his smuggling practices, basing them in Africa or South America."

"Until he took a wife and decided to set up shop on Grand Key," Joe said.

"That's what I suspected," Scobie said. "I gathered all the information on Morgan I could and gave it to Reeves. I tried to persuade Reeves that he and Mr. Watt were one and the same. But then, after Watt died, Reeves considered the matter closed—even though there was every indication that the smuggling was still going on. Well," he concluded with a sigh, "it seems his widow kept the business going."

"Why wouldn't Reeves do anything about it?" Joe asked. Scobie sighed and looked at the large man sitting in the dark lobby.

"You met Miranda," he said. "You saw how

charming she could be. Poor Jordan was head over heels—there was nothing he wouldn't do for Mrs. Watt.''

Frank nodded, remembering how beautiful Miranda Watt had been the morning they arrived on Grand Key. He glanced at Joe and knew his brother was thinking the same thing.

"I don't get it," Joe said, checking around the office. "There's no fax machine in here. How did she send the orders?"

"With this." Frank pointed to a phone line leading into the back of the computer. "She has a fax-modem. That allows you to send and receive faxes without using paper. Watt didn't want to leave a paper trail on her end."

"What a pro." Skinner nodded in admiration.

"She was cold-blooded, that's for sure," Joe reminded her. "What about that scorpion in my salad our first day here? She must have known we were Ambler's couriers and figured out we were trying to smoke her out." Joe turned to Officer Scobie. "That reminds me," he said. "You mentioned a tourist dying from a scorpion sting six months ago. Maybe you ought to look into the facts surrounding that case again."

"Let's not get ahead of ourselves," Fenton said, raising his hands to protest. "What's your explanation for the spear gun attack?"

"It was Miranda again," Frank said. "Last night she made a point of double-checking whether we still planned to stick around for a week. When I told her we were staying, she

146

must have guessed that we planned to do her in and take over the operation."

"Right," Joe said. "I bet she followed me to Clarkston's house and saw me on his computer. That would have made her realize that I suspected *him* of operating the smuggling ring. So she took Clarkston's spear gun and went back to the hotel. She knew that if she killed Frank with Clarkston's weapon, I would be convinced that Clarkston was the boss—and I'd go after him instead of her."

"The important thing is that Watt has been put out of business, permanently," Skinner said to Frank and Joe. "Good job, boys!"

"I second that motion!" their father added.

"Man, I am beat," Joe said through a yawn as he flopped onto his bed. "This has been one busy week."

"Tell me about it. At least Dad agreed to let us sleep over one more night." Frank was standing in the door to the bathroom of their hotel room, a towel wrapped around his waist. "A long, hot shower will feel great. Too bad we can't stay for a little more windsurfing—right Joe? Joe?"

Frank grinned—Joe was stretched out on the bed, already snoring. Frank entered the bathroom, closed the door, and was about to turn on the shower when he heard the door to their room creak open, then heard it slam shut.

"Joe, who's there?" Frank called. There was

no response. Sighing, he wrapped the towel back around his waist and opened the bathroom door.

What he saw made him gasp.

Joe stood by the bed, his hands raised over his head.

Standing in the doorway, her gun leveled at Joe's belly, was Miranda Watt.

Chapter

16

"BUT—YOU D-DIED in that explosion," Joe stammered. "I saw it with my own eyes."

Watt laughed lightly. "You saw what I wanted you to see," she said.

Frank stepped forward, his heart racing. "Was anyone in the boat besides Razz?" he asked.

Watt looked at Frank. "Don't worry," she said. "He was the only one on board. But then, he deserved what he got. I don't like my employees to break my rules."

"What rules?" Joe asked nervously.

"Razz knew better than to show his face near me," Watt replied, a harsh tone entering her voice. "I'd told him and the rest of his family—no contact. I couldn't afford to raise people's suspicions. Not that it mattered by the time

Razz showed up," she added dryly. "He arrived from Small Key a few minutes before you did, to tell me that the smuggling ring was finished." She laughed bitterly. "What do they say about the bearers of bad news?"

"But the explosion?" Joe persisted.

"Ah—that was one thing my dear late husband taught me. Always have an emergency exit," she said. "I knew the day would come when I would have to make a spectacular exit. An exit where everyone would assume I was dead—at least until I had the time to get far away."

"So you bombed your own boat," Frank said.

"Go to the head of the class," Watt said with a chuckle. "I've had my boat rigged with explosives and a timer for months. When Razz appeared here, I told him we had to leave the island immediately. Razz was to drive. While he wasn't looking, I set the timer for two minutes. Then I played the part of the hysterical, guilt-ridden woman, and told Razz I was going to turn myself in and that he should leave without me." She laughed a cold, bitter laugh. "The fool actually believed me. To tell you the truth, I think he was glad to be rid of me."

"But where were you when the boat exploded?" Joe asked, eyeing the gun.

"At your feet, my dear," Miranda said to Joe. "I hid in the cabin of the nearest boat—which happened to be the police boat. I almost gave myself away by laughing when Scobie, the old fool, shot his gun and believed he had caused the explosion.

"Enough of that," she said, snapping to attention. "There's one thing I need to guarantee my getaway."

"What's that?" Frank asked.

Watt smiled at him. "A hostage."

"Sorry," Joe said, shaking his head. "You came to the wrong place. We'd make lousy hostages—we'd always be trying to get away."

"I don't need you both," Watt said. "One will do. The other one I'll kill, to keep things simple. Which one should it be?" She looked from Joe to Frank and back again. "I think I'll take you, Frank," she said, turning her gun on Joe. "I have a feeling if I were to kill you, Joe would find some way to get revenge no matter what I did to stop him."

"Give it up, Miranda," Joe said. "You'll never get away."

"My husband did—many times," she countered. "He taught me what it takes to succeed. Hard work, determination, and a total lack of pity." She pointed the gun at Joe's head. "Goodbye, Joe," she said as she squeezed the trigger.

At that instant the hallway door swung open, banging Watt on the elbow. Her gun jerked to the left as it fired. Joe felt the bullet breeze by the side of his head as Frank dove for Miranda Watt's knees. Joe leapt forward and grabbed her wrist as Frank knocked her legs out from under her.

Miranda cried in pain as Joe squeezed her wrist. Her hand opened, and the gun dropped from her grasp. Frank scooped it up and turned to the door.

Malcolm was standing there, dumbfounded.

"Malcolm!" Frank said. "Are we glad to see you!"

"What's happening?" Malcolm asked in a confused, sleepy voice.

"You just helped us capture Miranda," Joe said, pinning one of Watt's arms behind her. The woman struggled against him in vain.

"She's alive?" Malcolm asked in disbelief.

"That's right," Frank said. "You caught her—and not a moment too soon. She was shooting at Joe. What brings you here?"

Malcolm scowled at Frank and held out his open hand.

"I just woke up and remembered—you still haven't paid me!" Malcolm said. Frank and Joe threw back their heads in laughter.

"And then he said, 'You still haven't paid me!'" Joe told a group of listeners at Marty Hausman's celebration party on his dealership floor in Yonkers. The showroom had been shined and waxed for the occasion, balloons floated everywhere, and the Hardys, as saviors of Marty Hausman's line of luxury cars, were the guests of honor.

It was only two weeks since Joe and Frank had returned to the States from Grand Key, but as Joe told stories about Malcolm, Miranda, Scobie, and Reeves, their adventure already seemed a lifetime away.

"Well?" asked Hausman's pretty young daughter, a girl Joe had never met before, named Marianne. "Did you pay him or not?"

"You'd better believe we paid him," Frank said ruefully, joining the crowd. "He ended up with ten times what we'd expected to pay. First, he charged for overtime. Then when he learned the FBI was involved, he tacked on an extra hourly charge for what he called 'risk conditions.' "

"We should have just handed over the fifty grand that Razz gave you," suggested one of the listeners.

"We would have split it with him," Joe said with a sigh. "But Agent Skinner grabbed it before we could. The whole package has been impounded by the FBI."

"Too bad." Joe turned to see the attractive agent standing beside him, listening in. "All's well that ends well, though, Joe. I understand Mr. Hausman is so grateful to you for rescuing him from financial disaster, he's going to make a special present to you at the end of the party tonight."

"Don't tell me." Joe glanced excitedly from Agent Skinner to Frank and Marianne. "It's the keys to a Jag, right? That black one in the corner over there?"

"I don't think so," Skinner said, turning to get a look at the sleek convertible. "It's something a little more—well, practical."

153

"Let me tell him!" Marianne broke in excitedly. "It was my idea. See, Joe," the girl told him, her eyes wide, "I thought you should have something more important than a sports car. I mean—everybody has one."

"Everybody?" Joe sputtered as Frank started to laugh. "But I—"

"Anyway, we thought we'd give you something with sentimental value—to help you remember that exciting night when you entered the car pirates' lair."

"It's a Mercedes?" Joe said hopefully. "Like the one we stole?"

"Not quite." Marianne glanced at Frank, who was choking with laughter. "Actually, I was talking about when you rode around with them in their van. The night you met them at the rest stop. Remember what you drove then?"

"Sure. I was driving—" Joe stopped midsentence, his face red. "Not a station—"

"Well, not the same one, of course," Marianne assured him. "But we found a station wagon so similar, you won't believe it's not the same."

"A station—" Joe sputtered as Frank howled with laughter.

"Buckle your seat belt, Joe," Frank said, patting his brother on the shoulder. "I have a feeling the New York highways ain't seen nothing yet!"

Frank and Joe's next case:

In the wilderness sport of orienteering, you have only three tools to guide you: a map, a compass, and your instincts. Frank and Joe have come to the mountains of Idaho to learn the game from a master, college champ Rob Niles. But on this particular course, the boys soon find out that there's only one instinct that counts—the instinct for survival.

A deadly trap has been set for Rob, and he and the Hardys are headed into treacherous terrain—a land of rattlesnakes, rock slides, and pinpoint sniper fire. As they blaze a trail to the truth, their courage, resourcefulness, and strength will be tested to the limit. Because if they lose their bearings, they may just lose their lives as well . . . in *No Way Out,* Case #75 in The Hardy Boys Casefiles™.